NO SURRENDER

BADLANDS BOOK 5

MORGAN BRICE

eBook ISBN: 978-1-64795-027-9
Print ISBN: 978-1-64795-028-6

Cover art by Natania Barron
Darkwind Press is an imprint of DreamSpinner Communications, LLC

NO SURRENDER

BADLANDS BOOK 5

By Morgan Brice

1

VIC

"Since when do serial killers get fan mail?" Homicide detective Vic D'Amato fumed. "How fucked up is that?"

"They don't just get fan letters; they get marriage proposals," his partner Ross Hamilton replied, shaking his head in disbelief. "I don't get it, but that doesn't stop it from being true."

Vic took a slug of coffee from his stained mug and barely kept from grimacing at the bitter taste. Hospitals and police precincts always made the worst java. "I guess it's like the people who follow all the true-crime podcasts. We get paid to be hip-deep in the worst humanity has to offer, but doing it for fun? People are weird."

"You've been a cop for how long, and you're just figuring that out now?" Ross teased.

Vic shrugged. "Every time I think that I've lowered my expectations too far, reality says—'Here, hold my beer.'"

"Yeah, well. I'm right there with you on this one." Ross chuckled. "Have you heard whether you and Simon will have to testify at the trial?"

"Pretty certain. Of all the charges, Fischer shooting Simon is the most ironclad, with plenty of witnesses," Vic replied. "I'm not in any hurry to be part of the media circus, but I don't see a way to avoid it."

"Lucky you—the Slitter trial is shaping up to be the biggest deal Myrtle Beach has had in a long time."

Vic grew up in a family of cops back in Pittsburgh. For generations, D'Amatos had been proud to serve. His father, brothers, and other relatives were still on the force up north while his sister was studying criminology. But an encounter with something supernatural Vic couldn't explain had made him unwelcome with the Pittsburgh police. Vic had relocated, started over in Myrtle Beach—and met the love of his life.

"I don't want to put Simon through what happened the last time," Vic confided.

"Not sure you're going to have much choice about it." Ross finished his coffee and set the cup aside. "The closer we get to the trial date, the more reporters will be angling for a scoop. I'm surprised there haven't been some camped out in front of the store already."

"I suspect Simon boosted the wardings against nuisance as well as malice. I tried talking him into going down to Charleston to spend some time with his cousin, but he flat-out refused to leave me here alone during the run-up to the trial."

"Alone—with me and the captain and the rest of the department, plus a squad of lawyers and witnesses?" Ross joked.

"And not one of you with any magic, in a trial where the killer used spells to help him get away with murder," Vic answered. "Simon doesn't want to be in the spotlight—or the crosshairs—but if it comes to that, I don't doubt he and his friends will come up with ways to protect us."

Simon Kincaide, Vic's fiancé, ran Grand Strand Ghost Tours. The boardwalk shop also offered psychic readings and séances, showcasing Simon's abilities as a psychic medium as well as his knowledge of the spooky side of local history and his background as a former folklore and mythology professor.

When an impasse in the hunt for the Strand Slitter brought the investigation to a standstill more than a year ago, Vic tamped down on his deep skepticism about the paranormal and asked for Simon's help as a psychic. Their first encounters with each other were prickly, and Vic accepted much of the blame for that since he had doubted Simon's abilities and hated needing his help.

Simon turned out to be the real deal, and his visions plus the ability to communicate with the ghosts of the Slitter's victims cracked the case—nearly costing Simon his life. In the year since then, Simon became an official police consultant, working cases with Vic and Ross when a supernatural connection seemed likely. Vic and Simon fell in love and now had a wedding to plan.

"Just because you and the Captain believe in Simon, that doesn't mean the defense attorneys won't try to make him—and us—a laughingstock," Vic warned, voicing one of his fears about the weeks to come as the trial played out in the spotlight. "Remember how the media sensationalized it before?"

"Not like I could forget." Ross rolled his eyes. "If it wasn't reporters talking about 'ghost whisperers,' it was the holy rollers shrieking about devil worship."

"We *are* in South Carolina," Vic said.

"I'm more concerned about the way the news has turned William Fischer into some kind of dark rock star," Captain Hargrove said, walking up to their desks with his coffee. "Like he deserves the attention. This is where copycats come from."

"Hey, Cap." Vic looked up. "What's it like outside? Still got groupies?"

Hargrove glared at Vic and pinched the bridge of his nose as if to forestall a bad headache. "Only you, D'Amato. Yes, your 'groupie' reporters are still blocking the sidewalk—which is public property, so we can't make them go away. I'd suggest going out the back way to avoid most of them when you leave."

"The last time I tried to sneak out the back, I got shot," Vic reminded his boss. "So I'll take my chances parting the crowd." He glanced at Ross. "Or we could feed Ross some bean burritos and let him plow the road."

"Pretty sure poison gas is against the Geneva Convention," Hargrove said with a smirk.

"Hey! I am not that gassy," Ross protested.

"Yes, you are!" Vic and Hargrove said in unison.

"Remember that stakeout last summer?" Vic asked.

"Or that time we drove five hours to the training class?" Hargrove added.

"Geez, make one mistake ordering lunch, and no one ever lets you forget."

Nothing about the current situation was funny, but dark humor was a police specialty.

"Jokes aside, I worry about the media coverage affecting the jury selection," Hargrove said. "Or causing a mistrial."

"Which would suck," Vic added.

"Look—we've got the best prosecutor in the state on this," Ross pointed out. "The case is as close to air-tight as it ever gets. We have witnesses to his attack on Simon, and we can put him at the scene of several of the murders. Let's not count ourselves out before the trial even convenes."

"I'm still bothered by the fact that it took a civilian—psychic or not—to recognize a pattern behind the disappearances and murders that we missed," Hargrove said. "I'm totally grateful for Simon's help, but it stings that we didn't spot the problem first, even if it took a while to find the answer."

"Myrtle Beach is a resort town—plenty of people in seasonal positions come and go all the time, and they don't often make friends who'll notice something is wrong," Vic replied. "So the only people who realize they're gone are their employers—who have their own reasons for not reporting the absences. Makes it hard to put the pieces together."

"Just makes me wonder what else we might not be noticing." Hargrove's expression and tone made it clear to Vic how much the thought weighed on his captain.

"We can't catch them all, Cap," Ross said. "We do the best we can with what we've got."

"Yeah, but we can try," Hargrove replied.

Vic glanced at the muted TV they kept tuned to the local news channel. "Hey, that's the D.A. on camera. Turn it up!"

Hargrove reached for the remote, and the volume rose, catching the interview mid-soundbite.

"—confident that we have a strong case and that William Fischer will be held accountable." Hamilton Andrews, the Horry County District Attorney, looked the part with his perfect blond hair, strong profile, serious expression, and a pair of "smart but not too nerdy" fashion-statement glasses.

"Are a psychic's perceptions admissible in court?" The reporter pressed. He was a short man with dark hair and a receding hairline, and the graphic on the screen identified him as Walt Baker with one of the local channels.

The D.A. wrinkled his nose as if he smelled something bad. "I assure you that various…investigative methods…were used; we have hard evidence that meets all legal standards."

"Any truth to the rumor that there will be a séance? Will the ghosts of the Strand Slitter's victims take the stand?" Another reporter called out the questions from the back of the group.

Andrews laughed until he apparently realized the reporter hadn't made a joke. "You're serious? No. Absolutely not." He looked out over the pool of journalists on the courthouse steps. "Good chat, everyone. We're done here for today." Several large men in dark suits stepped up to escort Andrews through the sea of people. The reporters jabbed microphones at him and held cameras to capture a glimpse as he passed, but Andrews did not answer their shouted questions or give a second glance to the photographers. Then he got into a waiting black SUV with heavily tinted windows and drove away.

The picture switched back to the two anchors, a man and woman who reminded Vic of the dolls his nieces played with, too meticulously coiffed to be real.

"I don't know about you, Amy, but I'm interested to see what the jury makes of having a psychic as a witness. Not everyone in these parts is comfortable with the supernatural."

"I agree, Trey. That's going to be a wild card. I guess it all depends on what role this ghost whisperer played in the investigation and whether the jury believes in woo-woo."

"Christ," Hargrove muttered before muting the channel as the talking heads continued to natter.

"Fuck." Vic glared at the screen as if it could pass along his sentiments to the news anchors.

"That's exactly what we don't need," Ross added. "But I guess there's no way to prevent it. Maybe they'll get the whole 'woo-woo' thing out of their systems and then realize how boring the real trial will be."

"I hope you're right, but sensationalism sells—and every channel wants to win the rating game." Vic knew his colleagues could read the disgust in his voice.

"Andrews is a damn good prosecutor. He'll do everything he can to keep the arguments on track and not let the defense pull a bunch of cheap tricks," Hargrove said. "And Judge Byrnam runs a by-the-books court. She's not much for lawyers who play to the cameras. We're going to have to trust the system—and hope it works."

Privately, Vic had concerns. *What if the publicity sparks a copycat killer? What if one of the Slitter's groupies comes after Simon to stop him from testifying? What if, after all the hard work and danger, Fischer ends up walking free?*

"I wish there was a different defense attorney handling Fischer," Ross put in. "There's a reason Hugh Wessell is nicknamed 'the Weasel.' Judge Byrnam is going to have her hands full keeping him in line, or Wessell will pull every dirty trick in the book."

"All of that is out of our hands, boys," Hargrove said with a shrug meant to convey indifference. Vic could read how much his boss cared in the hard glint of his eyes. "We did our job—now we have to hope the court can do right by the victims."

"Any chance Simon can get the ghosts to haunt Wessell and scare him into good behavior?" Ross's tone suggested he was only partly joking.

"I think you've mistaken the trial for that Christmas story with the three spirits," Vic bantered.

"Don't knock it 'til you've tried it," Ross replied. "It worked for Scrooge."

"I can't help feeling like we're waiting for the other shoe to fall after those creepy notes the prosecution received," Vic said. "Worded just right to feel menacing without making an outright threat. Whoever sent them knew what they were doing."

"And how to leave no traces," Ross groused. "Which is scarier than the notes themselves."

A week before, the District Attorney, presiding judge, and other members of the prosecution had received unsettling, anonymous notes. The paper, envelopes, stamps, and printer were so generic that they were untraceable, and they were freakishly devoid of fingerprints or DNA.

The notes read like disquieting fortune cookies, with ominous phrases that stopped short of actual threat. "Don't make long-term plans." "Are you sure you locked the door?" "Never take tomorrow for granted." The police instituted heightened security precautions, and the legal team tried to balance safety against paranoia.

"Alright, enough with worrying about the trial," Hargrove said, turning to refill his cup. "Back to work—unfortunately, Myrtle Beach still has other crooks to catch."

Vic did his best to put the Slitter trial out of his mind for the rest of the day. Hargrove was regrettably right—there were plenty of other cases to handle, none of them requiring magic to cause murder or mayhem.

Vic: *Things going okay today?* He texted Simon not long after they'd watched the news report.

Simon: *While I'm not a fan of the non-stop news about the trial, I admit it's been good for business. We've booked several tours solid, plus a bunch of private readings and séances. I guess people want to find out if I'm real.*

Vic: *Sorry?* Vic cringed. He wasn't sure whether to feel bad about the surge in bookings considering the reason.

Simon: *Guess we should have expected that this is what happens when you're internet famous. If we're going to put up with the hassle, at least we also get some paying customers out of it.*

Vic: *Any reporters show up?*

Simon: *None that got past the warding.* Simon included a slyly-winking emoji.

Vic knew that Simon's friend Miss Eppie had taught him several hoodoo methods for protecting the shop against evil. And that Simon used spells from a variety of magical traditions to reinforce the invisible safeguards on both the shop and the blue bungalow they called home.

Vic: *Be careful. This case is bringing the weirdos out of the woodwork.*

Simon: *You too.*

Captain Hargrove sent out for pizza rather than have anyone brave the pool of reporters who camped out in front of the department. Vic glanced out the window a few times and had to grudgingly admire their tenacity. He'd been on enough stakeouts to know how boring it was waiting for something to happen. Still, his empathy drew the line at breaking up that boredom by throwing himself to the wolves.

"These are for you." Ross tossed several envelopes from the day's mail toward Vic. "Looks like you lucked out on the junk today."

"Bill." Vic dropped his union renewal on the desk. "Crap." He tossed an insurance solicitation into the garbage. He frowned, looking at the last piece. The return address looked familiar, so he opened the envelope. "I don't remember ordering anything," he murmured.

"Springsteen's Glory Days tour?" The vintage concert ticket was difficult to find, and Vic was a true fan of The Boss.

He pulled it from the envelope and looked closely, eyes going wide when he realized the ticket was authentic.

"What's that?" Ross asked, curious.

"Something I didn't order—that's too good to be true." Vic handed the memento to Ross, who let out a low whistle.

"Even *I* know this shouldn't have just shown up out of nowhere. Is it your birthday?"

Vic shook his head and winced as his stomach gurgled. "No. Not my birthday. And I don't think the pizza is setting well."

Ross gave him a look. "Tasted fine to me. Drink a soda."

Vic headed for the vending machine, only to find himself running for the men's room and lurching into a stall. He fell to his knees and tasted bile, then lost the contents of his stomach into the toilet.

He kept heaving until everything was gone, and he was sweating and shaking.

"Vic?" Ross's worried tone told him that he'd been gone long enough to raise worry.

"Here," Vic rasped, not sure he was ready to stand up just yet, or that he was finished praying to the porcelain god.

"You weren't kidding about lunch not setting well. Do you need a doctor?"

Vic shook his head, then feared the movement might bring on another round of yakking up his guts. "I feel terrible."

"You look like shit—more than usual." Ross's attempt to lighten the moment fell flat.

"I need water." Vic decided not to chance moving away from the toilet.

"I'll get you some. And if there's a sports drink, I'll grab one." Ross disappeared, returning moments later with two bottles. "Go slow, or it'll all come back up."

Vic sipped water, only to have his stomach rebel. "I don't think I'm going to get out of here anytime soon. Go back to work. Check for my body before you leave for the day."

His stomach spasmed, and Vic dove forward, wincing as acid irritated his already raw throat. He rested his forehead against his arm, trying to ignore the bathroom smells that made him want to hurl even more.

Ross came back at intervals to leave more water and make sure Vic hadn't died, then left him to his misery. His stomach balked at anything more than small sips, and his whole body shook. He wondered if he had passed out once or twice. Vic wasn't disturbed, so he suspected Ross had put a sign on the door warning people to use another restroom.

"Hey, Vic—are you still alive?" Ross called.

Vic had lost track of time. "Barely."

"That'll do. C'mon. It's time to go home."

"Are the reporters gone?" Vic had enough presence of mind to not want to be seen like this.

"They're still out there. Want to make a run for it?" Ross asked.

Vic swore under his breath. "Yeah, but we are not running. We will walk purposefully with dignified speed." He wasn't sure he could manage navigating to the parking lot without help, but he intended to put up a good front.

Ross snorted, apparently not fooled. "Yeah, sure. Whatever you say."

"Alright, let's do this." Vic got to his feet without help, steadying himself with a hand on the stall until he was reasonably sure he wasn't going to pass out or throw up again. When a couple of minutes went by, he figured he could get to the car. Ross handed him a container of breath mints, and Vic nodded his thanks.

"I'll go in front," Ross said as Vic washed his hands, not wanting to think too hard about what he'd been clutching. "Stay behind me, and move as fast as you can. I'll try to block the cameras."

"What does it say about me that I'd rather face a madman with a gun?' Vic muttered as he and Ross approached the front door. The reporters spotted them through the glass panels and closed in.

"Detective D'Amato—"

"No comment." Vic held up a hand to fend off inquiries.

"Can you tell us—"

"No comment," Ross echoed.

"Just a short statement—"

"Did the Strand Slitter use real magic?"

"Will there be ghosts in the courtroom?"

"Is it true you're engaged to the ghost whisperer?"

Vic clenched his jaw on that last question as he and Ross shouldered through the crowd. They never paused, mindful that cameras recorded their every move, but they also didn't let the reporters hem them in or slow them.

"Detectives!"

Vic didn't look behind him at the disappointed shouts of the reporters as he and Ross finally cleared the small crowd.

"Whew." Vic exchanged a glance with his partner. "That was… not fun."

"Need a ride home?" Ross gave him a worried once-over.

"I think I'll be okay. I don't want to leave the bike here."

Ross looked skeptical but didn't argue. "Alright. See you tomorrow—so we can do this all over again," Ross replied, bumping Vic's shoulder.

To Vic's dismay, he found a familiar face loitering near where he'd parked his dark blue Hayabusa. "What are you doing here, Walt?" Vic asked with resignation. "Go home. I'm not giving you an interview or an exclusive."

Walt held up his hands in a gesture of surrender. "Hear me out."

Vic rolled his eyes. "Walt—"

"Hey, didn't I give you the tip about the truck that was used in the electronics heist? Panned out, didn't it?"

"Yeah, but—"

"And didn't I drop the hint that Jimmy Reno might be running the illegal poker club?"

"I get it," Vic replied, not entirely as annoyed as he tried to come across. As reporters went, Walt Baker was a decent sort. He fed Vic and Simon useful tips, knew which questions not to ask, and never edited video clips to be misleading. Vic knew the department needed some goodwill with the press, so he helped Walt out whenever he could without compromising his investigations.

"What do you want to know? No guarantee I can tell you, with the trial coming up."

"Is the Slitter Myrtle Beach's only serial killer?"

Walt's question caught Vic off-guard. It wasn't at all what he expected, and he was glad there was no camera because Vic suspected he gaped like a fish for a moment. "What?"

"People come and go like the tide in a place like this," Walt said. "Tourists. Drifters. Seasonal help. Locals expect them to leave, and no one asks where they went or if they got there alive. When they disappear, no one notices because they weren't *from* here, didn't have anyone looking for them. So how do you know the Slitter is the only one who preyed on them?"

We don't. Vic wasn't about to say that out loud, but Walt seemed to read the answer in Vic's eyes. *Dammit.*

"No one ever asked that question before, did they?"

Vic hated being caught flatfooted, no matter how much the question disturbed him. "We have enough work without inventing cases," he snapped. "Do you have proof? If not, you've just got a pretty theory."

"I have names of people who went missing over a year's time in 1982," Walt replied.

"Did they actually go 'missing' or just move on? Hard to tell in a place like this."

"My sources say they went missing. As in people who wanted to find them, couldn't."

"Sometimes people have reasons to disappear," Vic countered, intrigued but skeptical. "Good reasons."

Walt shook his head. "Not according to the people who missed them. Including my aunt."

That got Vic's attention. "What?"

"Her best friend came here to work a summer job in 1982 and vanished. She was close to her family, wasn't the type to run off with a boy, didn't have debts. But she was a waitress—summer help—and no one took the missing person report seriously," Walt said. "It's much too long ago to think we'd find her alive, but I think she and the others deserve closure. I've been digging into it, trying to find possible killers."

Vic's head swam with the implications. He knew that police were as subject to unconscious bias as anyone else. If the officers in charge back then had fixed opinions about seasonal help and were dismissive of reports because they thought they knew best, Vic could imagine incidents being overlooked and dismissed.

"What do you want?" Vic asked. Walt had positioned himself between Vic and his motorcycle. While he didn't like being ambushed, he still thought of Walt as one of the "good guys."

"Answers. Acknowledgment. And maybe a consideration to

change procedures that prematurely write people off because of what they do for a living."

That last comment made Vic wince. "Okay. Give me names, and I'll run reports. Serial killers are bad news. Do you have any intel on whether the perp is still alive? The ones you're digging into?"

He did the math in his head. If the killer was older than a teen in 1982, they'd be in their sixties now or older. Very possibly still alive. Juries often didn't like having an elderly person dragged into court for long-ago misdeeds, but opposition melted if the crimes were heinous enough.

"Not sure. I have some more leads to track down," Walt replied.

Vic nodded. "Let me know what you find."

Walt handed off a folded piece of paper. "That's a printout of my spreadsheet. Names, ages, all the details I've been able to track about the people who disappeared. Including my aunt's friend." He met Vic's gaze. "Thank you. I really appreciate it. This one's personal. I shouldn't have waited this long to approach you."

"No promises on what I'll turn up, but I'll give it a shot," Vic assured him. Walt stepped out of the way, and Vic got on the Hayabusa and roared off.

Vic breathed a sigh of relief when he pulled into the driveway at the blue bungalow he and Simon shared. He drove around the block first to assure himself that reporters hadn't staked out the house. Simon watched out the window as Vic walked up the steps and greeted him with a quick kiss.

In this light, Simon's hazel eyes were more green against shoulder-length wavy chestnut hair. He stood a couple of inches shorter than Vic, so he had to stretch to kiss him. His faded T-shirt clung just enough to flatter his toned, lean body.

Vic gathered Simon against him for a hug, loving how Simon fit in his arms. Vic's short black hair, dark brown eyes, and olive skin contrasted with Simon's coloring, as did Vic's more muscular build and the tattoos that peeked from beneath the sleeves of his shirt.

"You were looking for the press, weren't you? I heard your bike go past and figured you were checking." Simon chuckled. "I would have texted you if we had a problem."

Vic shouldered out of his coat and toed off his boots. "I know you would have. It's just been a long day, and I had to swim through the sharks once already."

Simon twisted the cap off a bottle of Vic's favorite beer and handed it to him, surprised when Vic shook his head. "I need water. Think I got hit with food poisoning this afternoon."

"That's weird. You've usually got a cast-iron stomach."

Vic shrugged. "Not today."

"I made your mama's stuffed shell recipe. It's in the oven and almost done. There's salad and garlic bread. Time to relax."

"Not sure how much I can eat right now, even though I swear I barfed up everything I've eaten since high school. But I'll try."

Vic loved how good Simon was at reading his moods and knowing how to nudge him out of a funk. Homemade comfort food and Vic's favorite brand of beer were a solid start to turning the day around.

"What was your day like—aside from all the new bookings," Vic asked as he filled two bowls with salad and retrieved the Parmesan cheese from the fridge.

"We got some new shipments, so Pete and I got those into the system and out into the shop," Simon replied. Vic knew how much Simon depended on his assistant store manager and fellow tour guide to keep Grand Strand Ghost Tours running, especially when Simon got pulled away to help with a case.

"It's the off-season, so the Boardwalk is pretty quiet," Simon added. "Which suits me fine. We've had more than our share of excitement lately."

"Heard anything from Dante?" Vic decided to skip the salad and helped himself to a slice of garlic bread. Dante was Simon's ghostly privateer ancestor who not only retained his memories but also his magic more than two hundred years after his death.

"Not today." Simon spooned a couple of stuffed shells onto his plate and grabbed some bread to go with it. "He drops in every so often, especially if there's a storm coming. Why?"

Vic shook his head. "Just wondered. If you didn't talk to any interesting living people, I thought maybe the dead ones had news."

"You say that like the afterlife is exciting," Simon replied. "I have it on good authority that it isn't."

Vic had taken longer than he now liked to admit to realize just how powerful a medium Simon was and that his abilities and visions were real. Just in the year they had been a couple, he had seen Simon's magic grow stronger and knew his fiancé had learned new ways to use his gifts.

The supernatural aspects didn't frighten Vic, but the dangers that came with knowing inconvenient truths and buried secrets sometimes kept him awake at night, worried about the safety of the man he loved.

Then again, he knew that Simon faced his own well-founded fears over Vic's job as a detective. Unfortunately, circumstances had substantiated their worry more than once.

"The stuffed shells are awesome." Vic picked at his food to stop his thoughts from spiraling. "You've got Mom's sauce recipe perfect."

Simon grinned. "High praise, coming from you. I'm pleased with how it turned out."

"It was weird today." Vic told Simon about the reporters staked out in front of the precinct and the vintage Springsteen ticket. "I still don't know where that came from. If I'd have ordered it, I'm sure I would have remembered."

They were quiet for a while, polishing off dinner before Simon spoke again. "There's a new ghost hanging around the store," he said without looking up.

"Oh, yeah?" Vic knew Simon wouldn't have mentioned the ghost if it wasn't important. He couldn't imagine the unseen world that surrounded Simon or having his ability to speak to spirits and help them find rest.

"Young woman, real skittish. Probably early twenties. From the clothing, I'd say 1980s. No visible wounds," Simon replied. "Although some ghosts can control how they appear enough to not be bloody when they introduce themselves."

"You say that so matter-of-factly."

Simon shrugged. "Have you ever listened to yourself when you and Ross get talking cop shop?"

"You've got a point." Being able to discuss disturbing information was an occupational hazard for first responders and medical professionals, and sometimes Vic had to be reminded that blood and guts weren't part of everyone's workday.

"She showed up for the first time two days ago, but she won't talk to me." Simon paused to finish his pasta and the last bite of bread. "I get the feeling that she wants to tell me something, but she's afraid. Which makes me wonder where her spirit has been all this time. Usually when a ghost has been hanging around that long, they've figured out how to interact with the living if they have something to say."

Vic frowned. "She's from the eighties?" That detail triggered the memory of his conversation with Walt. Vic walked over to where he had hung his coat and reached into the inner pocket for the folded paper the reporter had given him.

"Remember Walt?" Vic handed the paper to Simon.

"The reporter who wasn't an asshole?"

"Yeah. He thinks he's got a lead on a set of murders and disappearances from the 1980s that were possibly the work of a serial killer."

"Shit. Why would a ghost from back then make an appearance now?" Simon fidgeted with his water glass, letting Vic know the possibility deeply disturbed his partner.

"Do ghosts watch the news? The Slitter trial has been everywhere lately. People are probably talking about it beyond what's on TV. Could that rile up a spirit?"

Simon frowned. "Maybe—especially if there was a lot of discussion somewhere that had a deep emotional connection for the ghost, where her spirit might have stayed without making herself noticed.

Although it's more common for an anniversary to provoke an appearance," he mused.

"Well, you've got dates and details on that sheet," Vic said as Simon unfolded the paper and scanned the information. "Walt's been digging into this for a while. I told him I'd check the cold case records and see if any missing person reports or dead Jane Does showed up in the system around that time."

"If they were in the system, wouldn't someone have seen the pattern long before this?"

"Not if they weren't looking for connections. If they just wrote off the disappearances as young people being unreliable, they might not have taken the information seriously enough to notice."

"You'd think they'd pay attention when people disappear." Simon stared at the paper with a pensive expression.

"No one really disappears," Vic replied. "They don't go 'poof' and vanish into thin air." He winced, remembering some of the magic he'd witnessed. "Okay, not usually. Most of the time, it's because people stop looking for them."

Simon carefully folded the paper and rose to slip it into his messenger bag. "I'll see who answers if I try to contact the ghosts of the people on that list. It might take a couple of days for them to trust me enough to tell me anything—assuming that there's enough of their essence left to remember and that they aren't as scared as the girl is."

"Tread lightly," Vic warned. "If there was an earlier serial killer, then he could still be alive. Wouldn't be the first time we stumbled into old dirt that people would kill to keep hidden."

"We won't be getting a fruit basket from the Visitors' Bureau, that's for sure."

Their conversation dampened the mood, and Vic didn't want to end the evening like that. "C'mon. Let's watch a movie—something fun." He gave Simon a playful look. "I promise whatever we watch will have a very happy ending."

Simon smiled. "Oh, yeah?"

"Satisfaction, guaranteed." Vic leaned in and kissed Simon,

starting with just a brush of lips that deepened to slow and lingering.

They cleaned up the kitchen, then moved into the living room, settling onto the couch. Vic worried that he'd get a repeat of the afternoon's discomfort, but the problem seemed to have run its course. That still left him with aching abs and a sore throat. He had brushed his teeth twice, trying to get rid of the taste.

A fragment of memory surfaced, surprising Vic. "Huh. That's odd."

"What?"

"That concert ticket I got in the mail. I just realized that was the tour date they had to cancel because the band and the roadies came down with food poisoning. Weird, huh?" He rubbed a hand on the back of his neck, a nervous gesture. "I guess after that round of creepy notes the legal team got, I'm a little spooked."

Simon didn't laugh. "Yeah. That is strange. Let's get you better, and then we'll figure out who sent the ticket."

They clicked through streaming options and agreed on a favorite comedy/adventure they didn't need to watch closely. Vic wrapped his arms around Simon and pulled a soft throw blanket over them. With the only light coming from the TV, it was almost as good as a movie theater, with a lot more privacy.

Simon snuggled close, leaning his head on Vic's shoulder. His hand rested high on Vic's thigh, a gentle brush of fingers against Vic's cock that was far from accidental. For a while, they sat tangled up in the dark, as Simon's long fingers stroked along Vic's inseam, then traced the growing length beneath his zipper and slipped downward to tease along his taint.

Vic spread his legs wider and shifted to one side. He cupped the back of Simon's head as they kissed, letting his tongue run along his fiancé's lips. Simon opened to him with a quiet moan.

Simon's fingers worked at Vic's belt and then his own as the kiss continued. Vic mouthed his way from lips to stubbled jaw, kissing and licking down the column of Simon's neck. Simon kicked off the blanket, opened their flies, and pushed jeans and boxer briefs down until he could wrap his left hand around both of their stiff cocks.

"Feels so good." Vic's voice was muffled against Simon's skin. He added his grip to Simon's, and the friction of their cocks against each other within the channel of their hands was perfect.

"Not going to last long after the day it's been," Vic murmured.

"That's okay. Just taking the edge off. We can do it slow in the morning," Simon promised.

Pre-come slicked their palms, along with some lube from the container they kept in the end table drawer. Simon brushed his thumb over the knob of Vic's cock and began to stroke faster. They bucked together, savoring the slide and drag of sensitive skin.

"Simon!" Vic's throaty cry as he came seemed to push Simon over the edge as well, both of them spilling over their fists, panting with the intensity of their climax.

Hearts thudding, still breathing hard, Simon dropped his head against Vic's shoulder as aftershocks trembled through them.

"Love you," Vic murmured and used his clean hand to tilt Simon's chin up. Cheeks flushed, pupils blown dark with arousal, lips kiss-swollen, and skin glistening with a light sheen of sweat, Simon had never looked more beautiful.

"Love you back," Simon replied, moving just far enough to press their lips together again. "Feel better?"

"Oh yeah," Vic said, chuckling. He grabbed a handful of tissues from the box on the end table and cleaned them both up as the movie's credits rolled.

"Guess we missed the rest." Vic nodded toward the screen.

Simon gave him a wicked grin. "Not really. I'd say we got a perfect ending."

Vic turned off the TV and pulled Simon in for another kiss. "Let's change and wash up before we fall asleep here and wake up stuck together."

"Sounds like a plan." They made quick work of wiping away the evidence and getting ready for bed, then turned out the lights and slipped under the covers.

"Set the alarm early," Simon told him, his voice sleepy and sex-roughened. "Want to get your day off to a good start." He rested his head on Vic's shoulder, and Vic curled his arm around Simon.

They'd get too warm to stay like this long, but Vic appreciated a few minutes of quiet closeness in the dark.

"Counting on it, sounds like a recipe for sweet dreams." Vic buried his face in Simon's hair, breathing in his shampoo and soap and the smell of sweat and sex, resolutely refusing to think beyond the moment.

2

SIMON

Simon groaned when he saw the group of reporters staked out in front of Grand Strand Ghost Tours the next morning. He had kept his word to Vic and sent his partner off with a sleepy-but-satisfying sixty-nine to cure their morning wood, but the glow dimmed as he realized he needed to maneuver past microphones and cameras to get into his shop.

Before they spotted him, Simon changed course. He headed for his favorite coffee shop, turned up the collar of his coat, and got in line, scanning the crowd to make sure none of the press had stopped off for breakfast.

Tracey Cullen, the owner of Le Mizzenmast—which the locals called Le Miz—ran the register today, and her barista, Samir, pulled lattes from the large, complex, industrial-sized espresso machine.

"Good morning, Si—"

"Shh," Simon hissed, raising a finger to his lips as he came to the counter.

Tracey gave him a look. "You're incognito now?" Then she glanced at the TV in the corner with news footage of the reporters outside the police department, and her eyes widened. "Oh."

"Yeah," Simon replied. "Can you please do up four large lattes and a bag of sweet rolls, put them in a tray, and let me borrow one of those sweatshirts with the logo on the back?"

"Going into the delivery business?" Tracey smirked. Today her long braids were tipped with blue and white beads for a winter theme.

"I need a secret identity," he admitted. "Once I get inside, I don't have to come back out until it's time to go home."

"Coffee with a side of witness protection, coming right up." Tracey grinned and rang him up. "If you decide you want to order lunch, call me, and I'll deliver."

"You're a lifesaver," Simon said as he paid the bill.

"Happy to help—and keep you out of trouble." Tracey was the first friend Simon had made when he moved to Myrtle Beach, and he considered her a sister.

Samir had the lattes ready and the sweet rolls packed in record time. Tracey stepped away from the register long enough to find one of their delivery sweatshirts in the back and handed it off. "Good luck," she told him.

Simon flipped the hood up and took the tray with the food and drinks. He kept his head down, intentionally slouching and changing his gait. When he got close to the snarl of reporters, he held his breath, but they parted to let him through without comment, paying no attention.

Pete looked up when Simon entered. "We didn't order—"

"Yeah, we did." Simon closed and locked the door behind him, raised his head, and walked back to the small break room before shedding the sweatshirt and setting down the tray. He wondered if the reporters would notice that the delivery guy never came out—and what he'd need to do tomorrow to get by the pack that were dissuaded from coming inside by his wardings.

"I won't turn down a latte or two—unless all four are yours?" Pete joked, brushing a lock of sandy blond hair out of his blue eyes. He was in his early twenties—ten years younger than Simon and Vic—and still gave off a college student vibe, although he'd finished his degree.

"Don't worry—two are for you. And Tracey's offered to deliver lunch, so neither of us have to brave the scary reporters."

"I already called Mitch to see if he could get them to quit blocking the door," Pete replied, naming the Boardwalk Business Association's manager. "Customers shouldn't have to elbow their way through the paparazzi to come in for their appointments."

"No, they shouldn't." Simon passed Pete's drink to him and tried to relax as he took a sip of his own. "Good thing the nuisance spell Gabriella did for us makes reporters not want to come inside. The sidewalk is public, so she couldn't do anything about them hanging around out there, sadly. Did they hassle you when you opened the shop?"

"Not once I convinced them that I wasn't you. I'm not sure what they think you're going to tell them. It's not like you could talk about the trial."

"I imagine they're hoping I'd slip and give them a sound bite. It's not my first media clusterfuck." Simon shrugged.

He had lost his university teaching position in Columbia when a fundamentalist father objected to his folklore and mythology classes. He'd weathered that dumpster fire and the breakup with a fellow professor who feared Simon's "bad press" might hurt his shot at tenure. Simon had come to Myrtle Beach to recover and ended up with a new career and new love.

"I figured that I could cover your tours for a few days until the hubbub dies down if you want," Pete offered.

"Thanks. Let's see how it goes and decide. When's my first appointment?"

"You've got Lois McKenzie at ten for a private séance, three more appointments after lunch for psychic readings, and a phone call with Sally Anne Roberts at Grand Strand Sculpture Gardens to set up the Christmas ghost stories program."

Simon had written two books about local ghosts and urban legends and was working on pulling together a third. He was a popular speaker with the library and nearby museums, as well as historic places like the gardens that staged special events at the holidays.

"Has Ms. McKenzie been in before?" Simon asked, thinking the name sounded familiar.

"I don't think so," Pete replied. "I didn't get that impression from her when she booked the appointment."

"I'm going to check my email before she gets here." He started toward the office in the back and stumbled as pain stabbed through his temples. Simon barely managed to set the coffee on the counter before he staggered and nearly fell.

"Simon?"

"Vision," he replied through gritted teeth.

Pete came around the counter and steadied Simon, walking with him to the couch in the office. Simon sank down wordlessly and leaned forward with his head in his hands, trying to focus his attention through the pain, so he didn't miss what the vision was trying to tell him.

He saw a baseball game in progress, with players in old-fashioned uniforms. Simon wasn't a big enough fan to recognize the team, but he noted the colors and the swordfish logo. His view narrowed to the batter, a young dark-haired man with expressive eyes and a thin mustache who wore the number 12 on his shirt.

As quickly as the vision came, it vanished, leaving Simon shaken and his head pounding. Pete came back into the office with a bottle of water, Simon's abandoned coffee cup, and a couple of ibuprofen.

"Here. This should help. Lie down until your head feels better. I've worked with you long enough to know the aftereffects of one of your visions."

"Thanks. You okay up front for a while?" Simon swallowed the pills, drained the water bottle, and took a big gulp of coffee. Then he leaned back and closed his eyes, waiting for the headache to fade.

"Yeah. It's been slow so far. I thought I saw Mitch heading this way, so maybe the reporters will back off after he rips them a new one." The expectation in Pete's voice made Simon smile, despite the circumstances.

"Okay. Thanks. You're the best."

Pete pulled the door mostly closed behind him, leaving Simon in the near-darkness of the office. After twenty minutes, the liquids and pain killer kicked in, and his headache began to fade. Once the throbbing stopped, Simon could think again, leaving him to puzzle out the unusual images.

What the hell was that about? A yesteryear baseball team, and one player in particular. How does that have anything to do with what's going on?

Simon had learned that his psychic gift didn't always communicate in a predictable, linear way. Supernatural ways of knowing—visions, tarot cards, tea leaves, or any of the other many psychic abilities—didn't unfold like a book or a movie. Instead, they tended to offer a "highlights reel" of only the most essential, highly emotional moments, leaving the recipient to put the pieces of the puzzle together.

Normally, he loved the challenge. But the Slitter trial had Simon on edge, fearing that he or Vic—or their friends—could end up in danger. Catching the Slitter had nearly gotten Simon killed, and he was in no hurry to revisit that scenario. Simon worried that he lacked the patience to track clues and figure out what his gift was trying to tell him, even though he knew his paranormal insights might unlock evidence that could change everything.

Once he could move without triggering the pain in his temples, Simon sat at his desk and searched for information about the long-ago baseball team. He quickly turned up results about the Sarasota Swordfish, which had been a big deal starting in the 1950s but faded from view after they were bought, renamed, and relocated by a new owner in the 1970s.

"Javier Narvaez," Simon murmured when he found a photo of the same man he'd glimpsed in his vision, one of the Swordfish's star players in the mid-1960s.

"Narvaez's number 12 was officially retired as a tribute after a tragic car wreck shattered his right arm and forced his retirement from baseball," Simon read aloud from a post that showed up in his search results. "Why the hell would that matter?"

He realized that he had lost track of time when Pete stuck his head in.

"Feeling better? Ms. McKenzie will be here in about five minutes. Mitch went after the reporters like a bear with a bee sting and cleared them out—for now." Pete's tone made it clear how much he had enjoyed watching that spectacle unfold through the shop's big front window.

"Shit. Okay. I've mostly got myself together. Thanks for the warning."

Simon headed for the bathroom, where he splashed cold water on his face, finger-combed his hair into a semblance of neatness, and took some deep breaths to get himself under control.

When he emerged, he found a nervous older woman near the register, chatting with Pete while they waited for Simon. She looked to be in her late sixties, a slightly-built woman with a vibrant presence.

"Ms. McKenzie?" he asked, with a smile he hoped reached his eyes.

"Are you Simon Kincaide?" She looked wary, like she might bolt.

"Yes, I am. Thank you for coming. Would you like tea? Water? Coffee?"

She shook her head. "No, thank you. I'm a bit too nervous for any of that. How does this work?"

"We have a seat at a quiet table in the back, and you give me some information about the spirit you'd like to contact, and then I do my best to pass messages back and forth," Simon replied.

"Can I see the ghost?"

Simon had been asked this question many times. He wished he could give a better answer. "I don't know. Sometimes it's possible if the ghost is strong enough. Most often, no. It depends on a lot of things."

"Alright," Ms. McKenzie said, after a moment's hesitation, as if she were having an internal debate. "Let's give it a whirl."

"Please, come with me." Simon gestured toward the back of the shop where he had a table set up for private consults, separated from the rest of the store by a curtain and a folding screen.

Simon waited until his client got comfortable at the table. He sensed her nervousness and felt the psychic prickle that told him a spirit hovered just out of sight. "How can I help, Ms. McKenzie?"

Ms. McKenzie folded her hands in front of her. "Please call me

Lois. I've come about my sister. She went missing, and I've never been able to find out what happened. She's been on my mind a lot lately like she's here with me, and I thought I'd see if this really works."

Skepticism was normal—sometimes even hostility. People feared the unknown, particularly when it came to death and the afterlife. He knew that the many stories of frauds and con artists also made clients wary even after booking an appointment.

"When did she go missing?"

"In the summer of 1982."

Simon's breath caught. *That can't be a coincidence, not with that list Walt gave to Vic.*

"Have you ever tried to contact her spirit before?"

Lois shook her head. "No. It always seemed too final, like I was giving up on finding her. But after all this time, I know that she's gone, no matter why she disappeared. Even if she ran off. There was a four-year gap between us—she was my big sister. I'd just like to know for certain before my time is up."

"What's her name?"

"Alicia McKenzie." The older woman nodded. "Same last name. I never married."

I saw that name on the list. Damn.

"Please, take my hands." Simon placed his palms up on the table, and Lois took hold. Her thin-boned hands felt dry and fragile in his much larger grip.

"You can keep your eyes open—this next part is up to Alicia. I'd like you to please picture her as vividly as you can. Think about her face, her voice, the smell of her favorite fragrance, her handwriting. I'm going to close my eyes and try to sense her energy. If she answers, ask your most important questions first—there's no telling how long she can stay," Simon advised.

He closed his eyes and took several deep breaths, doing his best to relax and open his gift. The spirit who had followed Lois at a distance came closer but not yet near enough to communicate. Simon shivered as the temperature plunged, more to do with the ghost than the air conditioning. He studied the spirit silently, worried that trying to reach out too soon might scare the ghost away.

The ghost looked to be in her mid-twenties, with dark hair in a ponytail and a fresh-scrubbed, girl-next-door look. She wore a waitress uniform from a hotel dining room, complete with a name tag—Alicia—and practical shoes. Her sad eyes tugged at Simon's heart, and even though she didn't appear with her death wounds, he knew she'd come to a bad end.

Alicia came closer, staring at the old woman who was her younger sister.

"How long?" she asked.

"Alicia is here," Simon said quietly. "I don't know if she can become visible. She wants to know how long she's been gone."

"Forty years," Lois replied, and she gasped, letting Simon know Alicia was visible. "Alicia? I've missed you so much."

"Are you the only one left?"

"What about other family members?" Simon paraphrased her question, lending the spirit some of his energy to extend the contact.

"They're all gone," Lois said. "Except for grandchildren and nieces and nephews born after you went away."

"Not my choice."

"She didn't choose to leave." Simon turned his attention to Alicia. "Do you remember what happened?" he asked the ghost, worried that Lois might falter asking the hard questions.

"A pirate grabbed me and killed me."

Simon relayed the information, puzzled at the cryptic clue. He wished he could ask more questions, but he could feel Alicia fading, and he wanted Lois to have as much time with her sister as possible.

"I looked for you for such a long time," Lois said, her resolve faltering. Simon opened his eyes when he heard the tears in Lois's voice. "I want you to know that we looked. I never forgot."

Alicia's ghost nodded solemnly. She had managed to look almost solid, but now as her energy faded, the image became translucent. Simon had to ask one more question.

"Where is your body?"

"In the pirate caves."

Alicia's form blurred like mist in the wind, and her final words were almost too faint for Simon to catch before the ghost disappeared.

Tears streamed down Lois's face. She released her painfully-tight grip on Simon's hands as if she only now realized how hard she had hung on. "Thank you," she said, and while her eyes were wet, they also held a glint of determination. "You found her."

He handed a tissue to Lois, who accepted it gratefully to dab her eyes.

"Have you lived in or near Myrtle Beach this whole time?"

Lois nodded. "You're wondering why Alicia didn't haunt me sooner? I think she knew I wasn't ready to give up hope. For a long time, I couldn't let her go. But these last few years, I've lost friends and family—cancer, car wrecks, pneumonia. I realized that I needed to put my affairs in order—and that included finding out the truth."

She sniffled and blew her nose. "I knew, deep down. After all this time…I knew she was gone. We never believed she would have run away."

"Did you report her missing at the time?" Simon asked as gently as he could.

Lois nodded. "My parents did. The police told us that she probably ran off with a boy or moved to California to smoke pot. She was a young waitress from an unimportant family. I don't think the police tried very hard to find her."

She leaned back in her chair, twisting the tissue as she spoke. Simon thought Lois looked suddenly older with the confirmation of Alicia's death.

"We put up posters all over town. Offered as much of a reward as we could afford. People called with tips, and we followed up on all of them, but nothing panned out. We talked to everyone she worked with that last day. Nothing unusual happened. Nobody bothered her, no rude customers. She got on the bus at the end of her shift—someone saw her do that—and she never made it home."

"Alicia's ghost isn't gone. She just didn't have the strength to stay longer, even borrowing energy from me. If you give her a week or so to rest, you could talk to her again," Simon offered.

Lois smiled sadly. "Maybe. I'll have to think on that. Thank you. You gave me back my sister."

Simon shook his head. "She was always there—I just helped you make the connection." He walked Lois out to the register, and she turned to him at the door.

"Someone took Alicia from us. That 'pirate' killed her. I got my closure, but Alicia still needs hers. I know that you help the police on cases. If you can help solve her murder, that's the best gift you could give her and me."

"I'll do my best," Simon promised. He watched Lois leave, glad the reporters had scattered—for now.

"Either the AC kicked into overdrive or your ghost showed," Pete said when Simon turned away from the door.

"She showed—and left us a mystery. I think the ghost 'woke up' because of the Slitter trial," Simon said. "And I'm sure now that Walt was right—Fischer wasn't the Grand Strand's first serial killer. I believe Alicia McKenzie was one of that killer's victims—I've just got to prove it."

Pete handed Simon a candy bar and a bottle of water. "That's awesome. But if you don't eat and drink, I'll have to scrape your ass off the floor—again."

"Yes, Mother." Simon chuckled, but he appreciated Pete's concern and made quick work of the water and candy.

"Before you head into the office and go into Sherlock mode, remember you've got three readings and a call this afternoon. If you wipe yourself out trying to find old ghosts, those appointments are going to kick your butt," Pete warned.

Simon chafed at the delay, but he knew Pete was right. He drank his second, now-cold latte, admitting that the séance had taken more out of him—energy-wise and emotionally—than he expected.

"Tracey called while you were with Ms. McKenzie to find out what we wanted for lunch. Hope you don't mind, but I ordered you the ham and cheese and told her you'd need to refuel for the afternoon. She should be by any minute. If you eat fast, you might even be able to grab a short nap." Pete grinned. "I promise I won't tell the boss."

The bell over the door jangled, and Tracey walked in with a bag. "How'd your séance go?" She put the sack down on the counter. Before Simon could answer, she turned to Pete.

"One ham and cheese, one chicken salad, two bags of regular chips, two sugar cookies, a Coke Zero, and a Sprite," Tracey confirmed. "Since you paid online, the receipt's in the bag."

"Thank you," Simon appreciated not having to venture outside in case the reporters were waiting elsewhere on the Boardwalk.

"No problem. It's nice to stretch my legs. Did the ghosts chase the reporters away?"

"No, Mitch from the Business Association came down and gave them hell," Pete replied with a smirk.

"That works too." Tracey looked at Simon, questions clear in her eyes. "Well?"

"The ghost showed up. Murdered—never solved. Are there any caves around here?"

Pete and Tracey exchanged a look. "Caves?" Tracey echoed.

"That's what the ghost said when I asked her where her body was. Caves," Simon replied.

They shook their heads. "Not anywhere close to the beach. Hard enough to find places that can have a basement," Tracey said.

"That's what I was afraid of." Simon sighed. "Ghosts can be confused—especially when they die traumatically. Or maybe her killer took her farther away."

"Sit with it, and you'll figure something out," Pete advised. He pushed Simon's food toward him. "Eat. Rest. You don't want to faint on your one o'clock."

Simon retreated to his office and checked his mail and phone while he ate. He answered Vic's texts, letting him know that the reporters had been scared off—for now. Simon figured he'd fill Vic in on Alicia's ghost that evening.

Pete was right to caution him about not pushing too hard to find the ghosts, at least until his appointments were done. Simon chafed at the delay, especially since he still didn't know who the skittish ghost had been that he had glimpsed earlier. He wanted to dig into the list Vic had given him and see if any of the other potential victims' spirits would answer his call.

Simon knew that throwing himself into research was one way to deal with his PTSD about his near-fatal confrontation with the Slitter. While the nightmares no longer came as often, they still happened too frequently, leaving Simon shaking and panicked. Sessions with a therapist who specialized in military and law enforcement trauma helped, but she wasn't privy to the supernatural aspect.

The anxiety that had been a part of his old life at the university faded when he moved to the beach and reinvented himself. Encountering the Slitter had brought anxiousness to the forefront again, and when Vic had a close call and got shot, Simon found himself struggling more than he had for several years. He worried that medication would dull his psychic abilities, but fortunately, his friend Gabriella, a bruja, gave him potions that eased his tension without compromising his magic.

None of which seemed to be helping at this moment. Simon's heart thudded, and his hand shook as he gripped his drink. Slowing his breathing lessened the worst of the symptoms, but the tightness in his stomach made it difficult to eat no matter how much he knew he needed to refuel.

Simon ate half of his sandwich and finished his drink. He wrapped the leftovers and put them in the break room fridge, then went back to the office after a quick peek assured him the store was quiet.

Despite the food and candy, Simon felt the drain from the morning séance. He checked the time, realized that he could sneak in a twenty-minute nap, and set the alarm on his phone. The couch in his office wasn't large enough for his whole frame, but he arranged pillows and artfully slumped to fit.

Dreams of a pleasant walk on the beach with Vic gave way to a vision with the suddenness of a summer storm. *He saw a young woman dressed in a 1980s-style fast food uniform with a name tag that read* Lisa. *She looked familiar, and he realized she was the skittish ghost he had seen at a distance—only here she was alive and well. Simon tensed as he saw her get off the bus, show up for her shift at Leo's Ice Cream Shoppe, clock in, and joke with co-workers.*

From the light outside the store's windows, Simon knew time passed. When her shift ended, the dark-haired woman rode the bus back to the stop. Someone grabbed her from behind, but Simon couldn't see the attacker. Then everything went dark.

Simon fought his way awake, punching the air and struggling against phantom restraints. Pillows flew, and he nearly fell off the couch before he came back to himself.

"Boss? You okay?" Pete stood in the doorway, looking concerned.

Simon nodded, not quite ready to trust his voice.

"Bad dream? Vision?"

Simon held up a finger to ask for time and cleared his throat. "Yeah—still don't know who she is, but I saw our timid ghost right before she died."

"Did you learn anything?"

"She liked ice cream. Her name was Lisa." Simon took a deep breath. "Someone grabbed her when she got off the bus. I couldn't see who, and that's when the vision stopped."

"That's more than you had before." Pete had a knack for looking on the bright side that balanced Simon's caution.

The phone alarm interrupted them, reminding Simon of his appointments. "Guess it's got to wait until later. Better go make money to pay the rent."

Fortunately, the psychic readings had nothing to do with the Slitter or the long-ago disappearances. His clients wanted guidance to find lost objects and make decisions, hoping that his abilities could give them the information they needed. Simon knew that his insights weren't guaranteed, but they provided assurance and helped his clients make more informed choices. Their gratitude let him know how much that mattered.

"Go home," Pete told him when the last client left. "Don't take this the wrong way, but you look as wilted as last week's lettuce."

"That bad, huh?" Simon didn't doubt the accuracy of the metaphor since it described exactly how he felt.

"I can close," Pete volunteered, but Simon shook his head.

"Let's close together in case the reporters come back." Simon and Pete made quick work of it, and to Simon's relief, none of the journalists were in sight.

He had texted back and forth with Vic throughout the day. Although Vic and Ross seemed safe, Simon had the feeling something bad had happened that Vic couldn't share in a message. *Sometimes it's hard to tell foresight and anxiety apart.*

That wasn't exactly true. *Anxiety is seeing what could go wrong with every scenario. Foresight is knowing which path is most likely to happen.* Remembering that difference proved hard in the moment, especially when Vic's safety depended on it.

Simon insisted on accompanying Pete to his car, much to the other man's chagrin. "No one wants to talk to me," Pete protested. "I don't know anything."

"Lucky you."

Simon waved as Pete pulled away and then hurried to his car. In good weather on quiet days, the distance between the shop and the blue bungalow made a pleasant walk. That gave Simon time to let go of the day's hassles before he got home to Vic. With reporters on the loose, Simon had opted to drive.

Still feeling jangly, Simon took the long way home since he knew Vic wouldn't be back yet. Eluding the reporters had been a win, but he couldn't expect his ruse to work for long. Maybe the start of the trial would pull most—if not all—of the journalists off to the courthouse to ambush lawyers and jurors.

He drove by their house to confirm that no one was camped out nearby. Wardings and spelled protections kept those with evil intent outside the fence, but that didn't stop someone from loitering down the block.

The visions and ghostly appearances gnawed at Simon, leaving him feeling like he was putting a jigsaw puzzle together with pieces missing. Visions were almost never frivolous. The question was whether the psychic understood the meaning of the message. *Something about what I saw was important. But what?*

He still beat Vic home. Simon changed into a slouchy T-shirt and sweatpants, then made a cup of coffee as his thoughts swirled. The idea of "caves" bugged him, making him certain he was missing something that would be obvious in retrospect.

Without pausing to give himself too much time to think, Simon pulled out his phone and started down his contact list. Since coming to Myrtle Beach, Simon had built what he jokingly referred to as his "Skeleton Crew"—people with untrained and somewhat minor paranormal abilities. Without a mentor and surrounded by people skeptical of anything supernatural, naturally talented people often struggled with doubts, prejudice, condemnation, and incorrect diagnoses of mental illness. Often they became runaways and ended up in transient places like Myrtle Beach, where no one looked too closely at where they'd been.

Simon had made it a mission to find them and make sure they had what they needed to survive, including guidance in using their gifts and help avoiding the most common missteps that put novice practitioners in danger. His mentoring was casual and ongoing, acting like a big brother more than a teacher, although his university experience served him well.

Most of all, he wanted to protect those whose gifts had, until now, caused them nothing but pain, rejection, and fear. And to keep them away from those who wanted to take advantage of their abilities.

Simon's Skeleton Crew was spread across town, a fluid group, transient because they didn't fit in wherever they went. He hoped that while they stayed, he could offer training, affirmation, and a community, anything that would help them stay alive and have a chance to grow into their abilities.

Now, he realized that his network might be able to unlock the mystery of the "caves." It didn't surprise Simon that his calls went to voicemail—most of his crew worked hospitality jobs with varying schedules.

"Hi! This is Simon. I need to know if you've heard anything about 'caves' around Myrtle Beach. Call me. Thanks!" He left the same message over and over. Simon hoped that his question would spark recognition from someone who might break the cold case open.

When he finished, Simon sat back and rubbed his temples, trying to stave off a headache. "Fuck. There's way too much going on."

He needed a break, so after Simon put frozen burritos in the oven for supper, he opened his laptop on the table and sipped coffee as he waited for a folder to load.

"Wedding Ideas" included sub-folders for venue, food/catering, decor, and honeymoon. Every time he happened upon something that caught his attention online, Simon filed the link or photo for future reference.

Life hadn't given them a lot of free time since their engagement, and they had yet to set a date. Simon knew Vic would have opinions on some choices and not care much about others. He also felt sure that Vic knew Simon enjoyed the planning phase and left him to canvas the possibilities until the options had narrowed down to decision time.

Since he'd always loved arranging travel and vacations, Simon didn't mind taking the lead. They had already settled the biggest issue—where they *didn't* want to get married. A Catholic High Mass like Vic's siblings' weddings was out for obvious reasons. Simon's more liberal Episcopalian denomination sanctioned their union, but neither of them wanted a traditional religious ceremony.

Historic locations were too problematic to consider—this was the South, after all. Fortunately, Myrtle Beach had plenty of hotels with ocean views and beautiful ballrooms. Simon had arrived at a list of favorites and created a spreadsheet so he could sort by price, ratings, and amenities.

Just looking at the beautifully decorated rooms on the websites helped Simon shed the day's tension. He was still sipping coffee and paging through venues when Vic came home and paused for a kiss after hanging up his jacket.

"Get in a planning mood?" Vic teased, standing behind Simon's chair and leaning in to see the screen. "Come up with some good ideas?"

Simon tilted his head back for another kiss, sweet and lingering. "Plenty of good ideas—but it'll come down to price and availability when we actually figure out a date. I think you'll like a lot of these— modern, elegant but not fussy, great views, and good food."

"Food is essential for any D'Amato wedding," Vic said, only partially in jest. "No matter where we hold the rehearsal dinner or the reception, if my family rents a beach house—and they will— there will be massive amounts of cooking."

"Fine with me. I've eaten your mom's food. It's awesome."

Vic chuckled. "You think I'm kidding? I'm betting that Mom started planning recipes and menus as soon as we announced our engagement and put out the word to the rest of the family. Doesn't matter what we serve at the official meals—there will be manicotti and lasagna, half a dozen chicken dishes, and more cookies, pizzelles, and cannoli than you've ever seen."

"Just another reason I love you." Simon was grateful for Vic's large, loud, accepting family, so different from his own. After a major confrontation with his own mother a few months ago, Simon had no intention of inviting the Kincaide family, small as it was, to the wedding—and doubted they would attend even if he did.

"Are you sure your folks will be willing to drive all the way down here?"

"Hey," Vic coaxed as if he'd guessed the direction Simon's thoughts had taken. "One step at a time. Don't worry about anyone else—this wedding is for us. As long as we're happy with it—and married—that's all that counts. And yes, the close family will come. We don't need to have the fourth cousins twice removed."

Simon sighed. "I know. I just want it to be special."

Vic pressed a kiss to the top of Simon's head. "It will be. And remember what I said about the Chicken Dance."

Simon cringed. "Dude—we are not doing the Chicken Dance at our wedding."

"Pretty sure you can't be legally married without it," Vic warned. "It's tradition."

Simon once thought that the infamous Chicken Dance was an invention of children's shows and silly videos. Then he heard Vic's family reminiscing about family weddings and realized they were serious about it being a regional tradition.

"Just—no," Simon protested.

"What if I promise you the best blow job of your life between the wedding and the reception?" Vic gently ran his fingertip along the edge of Simon's ear and sent a shiver down his spine.

"It'll be our wedding night. I thought awesome sex came with the package." Simon couldn't give in too quickly.

"Oh, 'packages' will be 'coming,'" Vic promised. "I'm just sweetening the offer. It's a small concession since we aren't planning to get hitched in Pittsburgh."

"Oh, all right," Simon said with an exaggerated sigh. "As long as we can have barbecue and bourbon at the reception."

"I'll even let you bury the bourbon bottle to keep away rain," Vic said.

"How did you hear about that?"

Vic grinned and ducked his head, hiding an adorable blush. "I might have looked up Lowcountry wedding traditions."

"Oh, really? You know I'm from Upstate, not the Lowcountry." Simon had grown up, gone to college, and taught at the university in Columbia, the state capital.

"Yeah, I know. But we're both here now, and our friends are here, so when in Rome…"

"I think the hardest thing is going to be deciding on a cake." Simon clicked on a file filled with beautiful—and delicious-looking—cakes of all sorts.

Vic's stomach rumbled. "All of those look amazing. I'll be honest —I don't care so much about what the cake looks like as long as it tastes good." He slipped one hand over Simon's chest, and Simon reached up to twine their fingers together. Their rings glinted in the light, a sign of promise on the right hand, to be moved to the left during the ceremony.

"I don't care if we run off to a Justice of the Peace as long as when it's all said and done, we're husbands," Simon confided.

"You might not care, but my mother will," Vic replied. "Trust me on this."

The oven timer went off, and Simon closed the files and moved his laptop.

"Good timing—I'm starved," Vic told him.

They bustled around each other in the small kitchen like well-practiced choreography. Vic filled water glasses and set out silverware, along with salsa and tortilla chips to go with the meal. Simon took the burritos out of the oven and plated them, adding sour cream and guacamole on top of the bubbling, melted cheese.

"This smells amazing," Vic said as they both settled at the table. By unspoken agreement, they didn't talk about the stressful parts of their day, giving themselves a break to regroup.

Simon shared about the unremarkable psychic readings and recounted funny things that had happened on Pete's most recent ghost tour. Vic had stories from the other cops about the misadventures of criminals who hadn't thought through their crimes and made awkward mistakes.

By the time they finished, Simon felt much of the day's weight lift from his shoulders. But watching Vic closely told Simon that his fiancé was still preoccupied—a sure clue that something important hadn't gone as planned.

Once they had cleaned up the kitchen, Simon poured them each some whiskey and followed Vic to the living room, where they binged a couple of episodes of the newest superhero series. The longer Vic went without bringing up what consumed his thoughts, the more Simon suspected his worries weren't trivial.

"So what's on your mind?" Simon finally nudged, cradling his glass in both hands as he turned to sit facing Vic on the couch.

Vic took another sip and seemed to study the amber liquid for a moment before he spoke. "Hamilton Andrews—the D.A.—was in a bad car accident. Hit and run. He got sideswiped on the driver's side. Luckily, Andrews kept enough control to not get pushed into another car or something like a bridge abutment. But his arm is badly broken, and there's a possibility that he might have to pass some responsibilities to his staff attorneys."

"And that's bad?"

Vic shrugged. "Andrews is the District Attorney because he's got a strong record of convictions as a prosecutor. He has a combination of knowledge, talent, and presence that makes him stand out in a courtroom. That's exactly what you want with someone like the Slitter. High-profile trials have a showmanship angle—love that or hate it, it's still a fact. Bottom line—we have a better chance to put Fischer away for life with our best prosecutor."

"Shit." Simon knew that it was unlikely that the Slitter would go free after all the evidence and eyewitness testimony. But juries could be remarkably fickle, and Simon had learned from his partner not to take a conviction for granted.

"Yeah," Vic agreed and took another drink, savoring the taste. "I don't think the timing is a coincidence. First the menacing notes, and now this."

Simon raised an eyebrow. "You think someone staged the accident?"

"It wouldn't be difficult to set up," Vic replied. "But that's not the weirdest part. This afternoon—not long before the wreck—Andrews received a letter that contained an old-fashioned baseball card in an envelope that looked like it came from a club he belongs to. Except he didn't order the card, and as it turns out, the club didn't send it. Normally, no one would have noticed. But after those notes, we advised the team to be careful about their mail. He thought he recognized the sender, so he didn't hesitate about opening the envelope until he saw the card and realized something wasn't right."

Simon frowned. "Baseball card?"

Vic nodded. "Some team I never heard of. Sarasota Swordfish."

A chill ran down Simon's spine. "Number 12—Javier Narvaez?"

Vic gave him a strange look. "Yeah. How did you know that? You aren't a baseball fan."

"I had a vision. Believe me, baseball surprised me as much as you."

"What did you see?"

Simon told Vic all about his vision, the bad dream, and the séance. Vic listened with deepening worry.

"Then I looked up Narvaez because I figured he didn't show up at random. His career ended because he was in a car wreck that shattered his pitching arm."

"Fuck," Vic muttered. "That can't be good." He got up and paced, still carrying his drink. "Andrews isn't just a baseball fan—he's hardcore. The kind of guy who always has season tickets, who can rattle off all the stats. He talks about baseball all the time—it's kind of a joke among everyone who knows him. So whoever sent that card knew that—and meant to send a message."

"Where is the card now?" Simon asked, with an urgency that made Vic stop pacing.

"You think it's cursed?"

"That's a definite possibility, don't you think? Andrews is just fine; then he gets a card out of the blue from an unknown 'admirer' and has a mishap exactly like the one that stopped the career of the featured player? That's way too specific to be bad luck." Simon felt his worry ratchet up. "Like your Springsteen ticket and food poisoning."

"The ticket is still on my desk—but I didn't touch it today. Andrews reported the card as suspicious and had the forensics team pick it up. It should be locked up with evidence by now," Vic replied. "I can ask Hargrove tomorrow whether you could scan the card and the ticket for resonance. I know he wants to go by the book, and we were all hoping that the trial would be a slam dunk. Now, I'm wondering whether Hargrove even considered that Andrews's crash might have been more than an accident."

"Do you have any theories on where the card came from?" Simon asked.

Vic shrugged. "We've got some ideas. Apparently serial killers have groupies—people who write them fan letters and true crime enthusiasts who fawn over them trying to get details no one else knows. I guess most of the time the groupies are messed-up but harmless. But maybe one of them decided to help out their 'hero' by getting rid of the D.A."

Simon felt the hair on the back of his neck stand up, a clue that his psychic gift picked up on something Vic said. "And the lead detective?"

"Yeah. Is your Spidey sense tingling?"

"I think your instincts are good. Whoever sent the notes, the card and ticket—and cursed them—isn't totally random," Simon replied. "They're an 'interested party' even if they don't have any connection to the case itself. And if they're willing to use dark magic to affect the outcome of the case, they're not innocent."

"I just don't get it. Why would anyone find someone like that appealing?" Vic asked with an expression of complete confusion.

"There's a word for it—hybristophilia," Simon replied. Vic raised an eyebrow, and Simon shrugged. "I looked it up online."

"I can understand—I guess—people who want to be armchair detectives and read true crime books. Maybe they like the puzzle-solving piece of detective work without the danger." Vic's hand went unconsciously to lightly rub over the scars from the bullet wounds that had nearly cost him his life just a few months ago.

"That's probably true for the people who just like to follow along with the books and podcasts," Simon replied. "But it gets more complicated once someone starts reaching out to the killer to create a friendship or a romance. They call it 'Bonnie and Clyde Syndrome' after the famous bank robbers."

"Why would anyone think a guy who got off on killing people would be someone they'd want to know?" Vic sounded horrified. "Sane people should run away. Nothing good can come from having that killer's attention."

Simon shrugged. "Lots of theories. Some people want to fix them—redeem them. Some are attracted to the danger—they're the ultimate bad boy. Maybe the groupie considers themself so special that the killer would never harm them. And then there are the admirers who wish they could get the nerve up to follow in their hero's footsteps."

"You've got to be kidding."

"Hey, don't blame me—I read it on Wikipedia. I agree that the sexual attraction piece boggles my mind. But if you had someone who felt like life has been unfair to them, that they always get the short end of the stick, that people pick on them...they might fanta-size about having the power to punish people who hurt them."

"Like that's not creepy at all," Vic muttered.

"Creepy—and potentially dangerous," Simon agreed. "The more someone like that identifies with the killer, the more they're likely to start taking on their characteristics, trying to follow in their footsteps."

"Copycat?" Vic looked like he was going to be sick.

"Probably in some cases," Simon replied. "Most people are never going to get the courage up to actually kill like their hero. But if you've got a person who resents being powerless, maybe they see the killer as being strong enough to break all the rules and get away with it. Someone who deals with his 'enemies' ruthlessly. And if it gives them a boner too—well, bonus."

"Ugh," Vic replied with an exaggerated shiver. "Sounds like one of those crazy suicide cult leaders."

Simon nodded. "You're not far off. The groupies want to feel special and get their hero's attention. Maybe they want some of the fame to rub off on them. They want to make themselves into someone they see as being stronger, someone who wouldn't take the humiliations the fan has dealt with."

"That's scary as fuck." Vic rubbed his temples. "William Fischer was a monster who killed innocent strangers and enjoyed it."

"You don't have to convince me," Simon told him. "I was almost one of the victims."

"Okay, so when we look at the Slitter's fans, we need to find someone who might want to impress him or become him," Vic mused. "And someone who either has magic or has people around him—or her—who can be tapped for a favor, even if it's to cause harm."

"Which means there might be accomplices out there who may not feel guilty about helping him," Simon pointed out. "If you could find them and make them crack, you might get some useful intel."

"God, Simon. You sound like something out of Gitmo." Vic ran a hand down over his face. "Make them crack?"

Simon grinned. "Sorry. Too much TV. But you know what I mean. If someone who had enough magic to be dangerous but wasn't well trained got pressured into cursing the baseball card, they might feel bad about it. Maybe they'd be glad to tell someone in exchange for assuring their safety."

"You should have been a detective," Vic replied, deadpan. "You've got good instincts."

"And I talk to dead people, which can definitely help."

Vic finished off his whiskey. "Have you heard from any of the Slitter's victims? Or the people on the list Walt gave us?"

"Just two so far. I didn't have time today to do his list. Or, I should say, I didn't have the bandwidth," Simon admitted. "Tomorrow is quieter, so I thought I'd look at the people on Walt's list first. I'll try reaching out to their spirits. There are plenty of reasons they might not answer—and more than a few why they should. I think the shy ghost is one of them, and I'd love to get her story," he added and filled Vic in on the missing sister and the séance.

"I started looking at the list on my end to see what—if anything—had been done about the missing persons reports," Vic replied. "Shockingly little, as it turns out. I thought Ross and I might visit any close living relatives to see what evidence the police back then didn't bother to collect. I'm betting we'll get an earful."

"No doubt." Simon wrinkled his nose and polished off the last of his whiskey. "Just watch your back. Even if the cops back then have retired, you of all people know how common 'cop dynasties' are. Someone might not like finding out their grandfather was on the take or incompetent—and they might go pretty far to make sure nothing damages the family reputation."

Vic rolled his eyes. "Yeah, I can see that. I'll be careful. We have to walk a tightrope because, with the trial starting, we don't dare do anything that the defense could use to ask for a mistrial. And I want to keep the supernatural side of things quiet because—as you know—not everyone in these parts takes kindly to that sort of thing."

"Believe me, I get it."

Vic came back and sat next to Simon, then knocked back the last of his drink. "God, Simon—I just want this trial to be over. And I can't begin to imagine how you must feel."

"It's definitely making my PTSD flare up," Simon admitted. Vic reached over to take his hand, and Simon welcomed the connection. "But I'm more concerned about the new stuff—the cursed objects and Walt's list. There are some wildcards there we didn't expect, and I'm afraid they could knock us on our asses if we're not careful."

3

VIC

The next morning, Vic ushered Simon into the police headquarters through the back, but even so, they couldn't evade the gaggle of reporters waiting outside. They followed Simon's car but couldn't get past the guarded fence around the parking lot. That was still close enough for zoom lenses to snap photos, but Vic figured blurry images wouldn't make the front page.

"Hi, Simon!" Ross met them in the corridor. "I put a fresh pot of coffee on. It should be ready."

Vic gave an exaggerated sigh. "He doesn't make coffee for *me*."

"That's because you usually get here ahead of me and already have it made."

Simon chuckled, taking the good-natured banter in stride. "Let's look at Vic's Springsteen ticket first."

They headed to Vic's desk, where the vintage ticket sat propped up by his business card holder. Simon reached toward it and recoiled when his hand was still inches away.

"God, Vic. How could you not feel the malice?"

Ross waved his hand over the ticket, keeping a careful distance, and shook his head. "I don't pick up anything, either."

Simon shook his head. "Wow. It feels horribly *wrong.* It's not just dark magic—whoever sent this enjoys hurting people."

"Guess we need to lock it up," Vic said, wishing there had been a way to keep the memento—without getting sick.

"Make sure nobody touches it with bare skin," Simon warned. "If someone with latent ability handles it, they might get hurt. My bet is that the curse is specific to you—but we don't know that for sure." He looked to Ross. "I hear there's a mysterious baseball card in the evidence locker?"

"Yeah, Hargrove cleared it for us. Right this way." Ross motioned for them to follow.

The duty officer was expecting them when they reached the evidence room. "I'm guessing you're here for the card? You think it's hexed or something?" He regarded Simon with curiosity.

"Won't know until I get a look at it," Simon replied, and Vic thought his partner looked relieved that the officer wasn't giving them a hard time.

"Wait!" Simon called out when the man went to retrieve the card. The officer looked back at him, puzzled. "Do you have gloves you can wear? Just in case there is something wrong with the card, we don't want anyone else getting hurt."

"Sure. I can do that." He pulled on a pair of blue vinyl gloves, then returned with the marked evidence box, which he placed on the table. When he removed the lid, Vic angled the beam of a task light inside to give Simon the best view.

"Wow. That's the player who had a similar accident." Simon frowned as he examined the bagged card without touching. He held his hand over the box, palm down, and recoiled almost immediately.

"There's malicious power attached to the card," he told Vic and Ross. "I'm not a witch, so I can't give you details about the 'how,' but like with your concert ticket, I'm surprised Andrews didn't sense something was weird."

Vic and Ross tried holding their hands over the box like Simon had done and shook their heads. "I'm not getting anything," Vic said.

"Me, neither." Ross looked a little offended, like he felt left out.

"Interesting." Simon peered at the card under the bright light, but he didn't risk getting closer. "That explains why Andrews probably didn't hesitate to pick it up—it looked like it came from a familiar source, and he forgot to be suspicious." He turned to Vic. "You said he was well-known for his baseball obsession? Do you think he traded cards with people often? Or did he buy cards on a regular basis?"

Vic shrugged. "I wouldn't know—but his secretary might."

"Is the card valuable? I don't know much about baseball, but I've seen articles about collectors paying huge amounts for rare cards." Simon asked.

"Let me see what I can come up with," Ross said.

"How do we store the card so it's safe?" The duty officer looked a bit lost at the turn of conversation.

"For the moment, mark it as a biohazard and don't let anyone touch it or check the box out," Vic suggested. "And we need to bring in the ticket someone sent me—same treatment."

The officer looked skeptical, but he took the box away and slapped a big red warning sticker on it, sealing the lid shut.

Vic, Simon, and Ross headed back to the cubicle Vic and Ross shared, stopping to grab coffee on the way.

"If Andrews was a big fan, what are the odds that he was active in baseball groups on social media? Maybe under a screen name, since he was a public figure," Simon asked. "If so, the person who sent the card might also be in the same group. Maybe he was also a real fan, or maybe he was stalking Andrews. Because whoever picked out the card for him knew he'd want it badly enough to touch first and ask questions later."

Vic nodded. "Yeah. That makes sense. Especially if buying or trading cards was a common thing for him."

"Then we've got someone very dangerous on the loose," Ross warned. "The guy might have a psych ops background—if not, he's damn good at getting inside someone's head. Andrews took precautions. He knew he had a dangerous job. So someone figured out where Andrews might let his guard down and used it against him."

"Psych ops—and a witch?" Vic asked. "That's not good."

Simon stared into the distance, listening as Vic and Ross spit-balled ideas. "What's his game?" Simon finally asked. "That's as important as finding out who he is. Is he one of the Slitter's fans trying to throw the trial? Is he an accomplice who had a deal to spring the boss? Or is this someone with a bone to pick with Andrews personally—or over another case?"

"Andrews isn't dead, so we can talk to him," Ross replied. "He should be freaked out enough to cooperate—I hope. At the least, maybe he can give us access to his groups. We might be able to get a lead from the other members."

Vic swore under his breath. "Oh, Andrews will love that—giving up the one place he has a little space not to be the District Attorney."

"This was a warning," Simon answered. "He could have picked Roberto Clemente, and Andrews would have gone down in a plane crash. So our witch wants to throw a wrench into the trial, but he's not killing anyone—yet."

"Do you think any of your *contacts* might know more about this kind of thing?" Vic asked, uneasy using the word "magic" in the office. "Anything that might help us narrow the field?"

Simon shrugged. "I can ask. It's an interesting choice of attack. I'm going to guess it's 'sympathetic magic'—making one thing like another. Narvaez was in a wreck and broke his arm, which derailed his career. Andrews has the same kind of accident—and might lose out on a high-profile trial."

He frowned, thinking. "I don't get the feeling that type of magic is very common. That might be important. I'll put out some feelers and let you know what I hear."

"Thanks," Vic replied, knowing that he didn't need to remind Simon to be discreet. The last thing they needed was to have the press catch a whiff of "witchy stuff" regarding Andrews's incident or the trial. There had already been enough pointed comments by some of the state's more religious lawmakers that using psychics or mediums to help with cases was akin to making a deal with the devil.

"Don't worry," Simon said with a wry smile as if he guessed Vic's thoughts. "I'll keep it quiet. Trust me—the 'community' doesn't want the press poking around any more than you do." Vic knew Simon meant the others with paranormal abilities as well as the local witches.

"While you're here—I ran those names Walt gave me through the system." Vic beckoned Ross and Simon over to his computer. "Most of them had official missing persons reports on file. A few didn't, which either means the police talked the family out of filing, or for some reason they didn't try."

"Or they didn't have families," Ross said. "Wasn't that part of the Slitter's pattern? He looked for people on work visas who wouldn't be missed."

Vic nodded. "Yeah—most of the time. The ones on Walt's list weren't on visas. But they were young women who came to Myrtle Beach from small towns to work hospitality jobs. Most of them hadn't been in town for a full year. So they were inexperienced and vulnerable. Easy pickings." He knew the others could hear in his tone how much he despised people who took advantage of others' weaknesses.

"With everything that happened yesterday, I didn't have a chance to look into the list the way I want to," Simon admitted. "I have a slow day today at the store. I thought I'd start working my way through the list and see who answers."

Vic gave him a worried look. "Just don't push yourself too hard. The disappearances were long enough ago that we're not going to rescue anyone, and the odds are against us finding the killer. So you don't have to make yourself sick by trying to do too much, too quickly." He hoped Simon read the worry in his tone for concern instead of assuming Vic didn't trust him.

"I'll be careful."

"You're going to do that at the store? Where Pete's around to call if you faceplant?" Vic asked.

"I figured you'd prefer that." Simon couldn't help smiling at Vic's protectiveness.

"Damn right," Vic muttered.

"D'Amato, Hamilton—and you, too, Kincaide. We've got another situation." Captain Hargrove strode up with a look on his face that made the cops in his wake move out of his way.

"What's up, Cap?" Vic turned so he could try to read Hargrove's expression. He knew that the grim set of the man's jaw and hard look in his eyes couldn't mean anything good.

"Judge Byrnam had a heart attack. Coincidentally, she got an unsolicited item in the mail, and because of all those spooky notes, she asked her secretary to send it to the police before she collapsed. Now she's in the hospital," Hargrove fretted. "What do you know about poker?"

Vic and the others exchanged a glance at the non-sequitur. "Poker?" Ross echoed.

"The judge is a big poker fan—blames it on growing up with four brothers. Loves watching tournaments, plays a mean hand in charity competitions, and reportedly has an annual trip to Vegas with her law school pals," Hargrove said.

"Let me guess—the judge received a poker chip right before the incident?" Simon guessed.

Hargrove gave a curt nod. "Yep. Got it in one," he said. "It's 'mild' as heart attacks go, but she's in the hospital under observation, and this is likely to push back the trial date. If it turns out to be serious enough, they might assign a new judge, and that would fuck up everything."

"Shit," Vic muttered. "Here's hoping the judge bounces back quickly."

"Can I see the poker chip?" Everyone looked at Simon. "If it's like the baseball card, then it's also a message."

"You think it's significant?" Hargrove asked.

Simon nodded. "I had a vision about the baseball card. Then when I looked it up, the player's career ended when a car crash broke his arm. Just like what happened to the D.A. Now, the judge and the poker chip. I think someone is cursing people related to the trial—and using something that ties into their favorite interests to make the trigger item irresistible."

"Shit. That should sound totally wacko—but it doesn't. And the poker chip is being processed with the other evidence after forensics picked it up, but I took a picture since I figured you were going to ask." Hargrove dug his work phone out of his pocket, pulled up the photo, and handed the device to Simon.

"Pokeriffic Championship—Las Vegas 2001," Simon read aloud from the gold imprint on the chip. "Someone want to do a search on that? Try 'Pokeriffic 2001 heart attack' for starters."

"On it," Ross replied, fingers flying on his keyboard. A minute later, he looked up in triumph. "Got something!"

Ross turned his screen so that the others could see. A list of results all repeated the same headline, *Poker Champ Sidelined by Heart Attack*.

"Sid Osterman, ten-time Poker Grand Poohbah and the favorite of oddsmakers to be the next Pokeriffic Champion was forced to withdraw from the tournament when a heart attack sent him reeling in the middle of a playoff game," Ross narrated.

"He doesn't die—at least according to these articles—but it cost him the win."

"Fuck this," Hargrove rumbled. "We've got a stalker who's gone from ominous notes to sending items that not only show an unsettling knowledge of the target's personal life but imply a threat. They learn as much as they can about their targets, then send them something they can't resist."

"Then—wham! Bad mojo takes them out of play," Vic added.

Simon nodded. "The baseball card definitely held malicious energy," he confirmed. "As I told Vic and Ross, I'm not a witch, so I can't tell you for sure what sort of magic was used, but I've got friends who are practitioners of the craft I can ask to look into it."

"The craft?" Hargrove echoed, looking out of his element.

"Witches," Vic replied. "He means witches."

"Good," the captain said without missing a beat. "Thank fuck someone knows who to call."

Vic felt a surge of gratitude to have a captain who not only could accept the existence of the supernatural but was willing to allow people with gifts he didn't fully understand to help when it meant solving a tough case.

"I'll let you know what I hear as soon as I have something," Simon promised.

"This is not what they taught at the Academy," Hargrove admitted. "We didn't cover hexes and curses. If I hadn't seen some of this stuff myself, I wouldn't believe it. So we need to be careful because if the media gets wind of the whole 'curse' thing, they'll roast us, and it will play against us with the Slitter trial."

"I think that's exactly what the person who's doing this is counting on," Vic said. "Sooner or later, this is going to take on the 'Curse of King Tut's Tomb' angle with the media, especially with the strange anonymous gifts. Once poison is ruled out, what's left? They can't even say it's 'psychosomatic' because heart attacks and car wrecks are not imagined. And once we jump the shark, we've lost credibility."

"Even when the shark is real," Ross pointed out.

"That's why I'm counting on the three of you to figure out a way to save our asses on this," Hargrove said. "It's totally unfair and unrealistic, but I need you to help us. You're our only hope."

"Shouldn't there be a robot and a hologram to go with that?" Ross asked, keeping his expression innocent.

"You have watched that movie too many times, geek boy," Vic teased.

Hargrove scrubbed a hand down over his face. "I really don't know how I'm going to buy us time, so whatever you can come up with—as fast as you find it—I'm grateful. We are the firewall to keep this trial from falling apart."

Yeah, no pressure.

"Thanks for coming to look at the card and the ticket," Vic told Simon as he walked him to the door. "I know it was jarring."

Simon shrugged. "I don't know that I'd put it quite like that— the sensation of the malicious magic wasn't comfortable, but it also —thank God—wasn't personal. When you get the poker chip, call me, and I'll come have a look, although I suspect it'll be much the same."

"I think you're right. So we need to find this person before they manage to tank the whole trial," Vic agreed.

Vic leaned in for a quick kiss at the back door and insisted on walking Simon to his car, even though the paparazzi hung on the chain-link fence and yelled questions, brandishing boom mics and sporting telephoto lenses.

Simon and Vic disregarded the noise. Vic couldn't help thinking that he had numerous impolite hand gestures he'd like to share with the crowd, but Simon brought his palm down on Vic's shoulder in warning, as if Simon had guessed his fiancé's intention.

"Call me after you get in," Vic warned. "If there are people blocking the entrance, let me know, and I'll send a squad car."

"I promise," Simon said solemnly. "And I need you to be upfront if anyone mails another suspicious package. Don't forget—you're still on the witch's hit list. Come home safely. I'm planning on a nice, quiet dinner."

Vic thought of how often their meals had been interrupted of late. "I intend to do my best to make sure we can have the evening all to ourselves."

"I'm counting on it," Simon said with a grin, waving as he got into his car and drove away.

"I recognize that look in your eyes," Ross said when Vic came back to his desk. "You're looking for trouble."

"Not really. But I do think we should go pay Hamilton Andrews a professional visit."

Ross sighed. "I figured as much. I've floated the idea with Hargrove, and he gave permission—provided we 'tread carefully.' Which I took to mean no asking whether he knows who cursed him."

"Geez, Ross. Give me some credit. I can be subtle."

"As a baseball bat," Ross muttered. "Just remember—Andrews doesn't buy into the woo-woo stuff."

"We don't need to speculate about the card having anything to do with the accident. It's clearly a threat—sent by someone who knew it would be irresistible for him. I want to crack his contacts list. And when Judge Byrnam is well enough, do the same for her. If we overlay their contacts, sooner or later we'll find people in common," Vic replied.

Ross perched on the edge of his desk. "I doubt the sender would be dumb enough to use the same name in a baseball fan group that he'd use in a group for poker enthusiasts."

Vic shrugged. "That's where we let the tech guys go to town on the information—they can find IP addresses and shit like that. The crazy fan might think about using different online names, but most people don't know how to spoof the techie stuff."

"Let's give it a shot and see where it gets us." Ross grabbed his phone, ready to go, and shot Vic a puzzled glance when he saw his partner typing on his computer.

"I'll be ready in a minute," Vic said. "I wanted to submit a request for the cold case files on the disappearances from back in the eighties. There might not be much to go on—but you never know." He filled in the rest of the form and hit enter. Then he slipped into his jacket and shoved his phone into his pocket.

"C'mon. I'll get the car. We can get some officers to plow the road for us, move the reporters out of the way."

To Vic's relief, the reporters didn't try to follow them. He kept an eye out for a tail, but he trusted Ross's evasive driving skills. This was far from their first rodeo.

They pulled up in front of a nice home in a gated North Myrtle Beach community. "Glad we called ahead. Wouldn't have wanted to ram the gates," Vic observed.

"Just because you can't see the machine gun towers doesn't mean they aren't here," Ross joked. "They're camouflaged as decorative lighthouses."

Vic glanced at the replica tower near the front entrance. "You might be right about that."

A middle-aged woman opened the door. "I'm Kathleen, the housekeeper. Mr. Andrews is in the living room." She gave them a disapproving once-over. "He's still recovering. I trust you'll keep that in mind."

Kathleen led them to the sitting room, where Hamilton Andrews sat in a recliner, resting his cast on the arm. He didn't look at all like his court persona. His perfect hair—something the media frequently mentioned—looked like a bird's nest. He had dark circles under his eyes and bruises on his face from the airbag.

"Vic and Ross. To what do I owe the honor—since as I recall, you work the homicide beat, and as you can see, I'm very much alive." He gestured toward the couch across from him, managing to wiggle his fingers in the cast that encased his right arm from elbow to mid-palm.

"We're glad to see that, Hamilton. We have a few questions, and we appreciate you taking time to see us," Ross replied, taking the lead.

"What do you want to know that I haven't already told the police?"

Vic smiled. "Someone knew that baseball card would be catnip for you. We think one of the Slitter's fanboys is stalking people important to the case. You've heard about Judge Byrnam?"

Andrews nodded. "Yes. But surely you don't think a heart attack is related?"

"Did they tell you she received a poker chip from a tournament where the lead player had to forfeit because he had a heart attack?" Vic asked. "And right before your accident, I got a vintage Springsteen ticket in the mail from the concert they canceled because of food poisoning—and got violently ill."

A look of alarm crossed Andrews's face before his court-honed acting skills kicked in. "How could the card or ticket or a poker chip have anything to do with what happened?"

Ross cleared his throat. "We don't quite have the 'how' figured out. So we're working on the 'who.' Are you active in any online or in-person groups for baseball fans?"

"Surely you don't think—"

"We don't know what to think, Hamilton. So we have to eliminate the possibilities until we find the right one," Vic replied. "I'm betting you're part of some online groups where you can be a 'regular Joe' behind a screen name. That same anonymity hides someone who *does* know who you are and figured out how to bait the hook."

"I'm not superstitious, but I do see the parallel with Narvaez and my car accident. Although I have no idea how someone would pull that off. Your boys arrested the driver who hit me. You think he sent me the card and then made the crash happen? Why would he do that? He's in jail now—not exactly a winning strategy."

Vic shook his head. "I don't think the driver sent the card—or the ominous note from before. I'm not sure how he became involved. We have a theory that one of the Slitter's fans is somehow behind both the card you received and Judge Byrnam's poker chip. If we can find out who he is, we can figure out the 'how' later."

The look on Andrews's face made it clear he hated giving up details on his off-hours diversion. "I guess this means you're going to get a subpoena for the group administrators to get the membership information. You'll have to explain your reason. I won't be able to go back."

"You could change your screen name," Ross offered.

Andrews shook his head. "I've been a member for years. They'd recognize how I sound in my posts, even under a different name. I know it's not important in the grand scheme of things, but it pisses me off to lose that. Having fun and just enjoying a hobby gets tricky when people see your face on TV."

"Price of fame?" Vic replied, only partially in jest.

Andrews snorted. "Yeah, I guess so. My group name is DiMaggioFan. My grandfather worshipped that guy."

"Were there any interactions you had in the group that made you uncomfortable or that seemed odd?" Ross asked. "Maybe someone who seemed a little too eager to be your friend?"

Andrews thought for a moment. "I don't know if you participate in any groups, but it's pretty common for there to be a small core of very active members, no matter how many people are technically in the club. Not to say the sender couldn't have been lurking, but ego is often a big thing with stalkers. They're playing a mental game and want to see how close they can come without getting caught. In their mind, they're all Moriarty."

"Interesting," Ross mused. He looked at Vic. "That means we start with the fifty most active members and go from there."

"We want to cross-reference the IP addresses between your groups and Judge Byrnam's," Vic said. "I've got a suspicion that the overlap between the groups will be our guy."

Andrews nodded. "I think you're on to something, detective. Nice work."

"Captain Hargrove put out a warning to anyone involved in the trial to be wary of unexpected letters or packages from unknown senders. It was heavy on caution and light on details, but we're hoping people will think twice before opening mail from people they don't know," Ross put in.

Andrews gave them an appraising look. "You think there's something supernatural going on."

"Maybe," Vic allowed. "We're leaving all possibilities open."

"Did you have your psychic friend take a look at the card and your ticket?" Andrews's tone was less mocking than Vic might have expected.

Vic hesitated before nodding. "He picked up malicious energy on it and the ticket—and we're expecting the same with the poker chip. That's not a surprise. The question is—was someone able to harness that power to cause real harm?"

"In other words, magic."

Vic shrugged again, trying to deflect. "We're early in our investigation."

Andrews cocked his head and gave Vic a "don't bullshit me" look. "Uh-huh."

"Do you have a theory?" Ross asked, and Vic knew his partner was trying to diffuse the situation.

Andrews barked a bitter laugh. "It's a damned inconvenient coincidence, which makes me doubt that it's as coincidental as it looks. To tell you the truth, it's kinda freaky. I don't like thinking that magic might be real. But I've seen what master manipulators can do to people, and it certainly qualifies as 'putting them under a spell.' So—unofficially, off the record—I'm willing to keep an open mind."

Vic let out a sigh of relief. "Thank you. We're being discreet. We don't want this to turn into a media circus." He hesitated. "I've got another question. Were there ever rumors about Myrtle Beach having a serial killer before the Slitter?"

Andrews looked surprised, then just as quickly schooled his features. "Why do you ask?"

"We think there was a series of deaths and disappearances back in the eighties that might have been overlooked," Ross said. "The visibility of the Slitter trial has brought some old unfinished business to light."

"Interesting. Wouldn't surprise me. People tend to avoid seeing disturbing patterns—especially when it's bad for business," Andrews replied. "Step carefully. You know who runs this town. They can be very protective when it comes to bad news that might keep people from vacationing here."

"Understood," Vic replied with a nod. Real estate developers ran Myrtle Beach—that was no secret. Visionary land developers and railroad men created the Grand Strand as a way to optimize their beachfront property in the booming Post War period. Myrtle Beach was something of an artificial construct—a planned town rather than one which sprang up naturally. Those same families remained quietly powerful in local affairs since they owned much of the most valuable land.

Andrews looked tired, and Vic didn't want to overstay their welcome. Andrews was a valuable ally, and keeping him on their side made life a lot easier.

"What did you make of that?" Ross asked as they drove back to the office.

"What happened rattled him," Vic replied, watching the town pass out the passenger window. "He's all law and logic, and he's weirded out because he senses something is sketchy about this, but he can't explain it."

"He didn't throw us out. That's a plus."

"Nothing like low expectations," Vic joked.

"It beats having none at all," Ross returned. "So what's the next move? We're not going to be able to get in to see the judge for a while."

"We can't wait for the perp to send out more cursed objects," Vic replied. "So I thought maybe we can make him come to us."

Ross risked a glance at Vic. "Don't tell me you intend to use yourself as bait. Simon will make sure my ass gets haunted for eternity if anything happens to you."

"I'll make sure it doesn't get that far. We just want to force his hand, flush him out," Vic replied, thinking aloud. "Let him think that he failed with the ticket, goad him into trying again."

"I know I'm going to regret this, but what did you have in mind?"

"I'll drop in on the Springsteen fan groups that I rarely visit, and burn up the chat talking about the cool vintage ticket, make like nothing weird happened. If our guy is out there, he's going to wonder why the curse didn't stick. Gives our IT guys another data set for comparison."

"Did you discuss this with Simon?"

"I just thought of it while we were talking to Andrews," Vic admitted.

"Yeah. I'm gonna get haunted for sure."

"I'm not making anything new happen. You know Simon and I are already on the perp's list. I'm just making him doubt himself. He might make mistakes or not cover his tracks."

"You're afraid he'll go after Simon next." Ross didn't make it a question.

Vic looked away, giving Ross his answer.

"Simon's the one who's going to figure out how to break the curse," Vic said after a pause. They had pulled into the station's lot a while ago but weren't ready to continue their conversation in a more public place.

"I have no intention of getting hurt. But if I do, you and Hargrove will be able to carry on. If something happens to Simon

—" Vic cleared his throat. "His friends might be able to figure it out, but it'll take them longer. He's onto something about the other murders in the eighties. I'm sure it all ties together. We need him. I'm—"

"Do not say 'expendable,'" Ross warned. "I'd have to kick your ass."

Vic gave him a look. "That wasn't what I was going to say. More like 'replaceable'—in the short term," he hurried to add. "I can be benched, and the rest of the team can still win. We can't replace Simon's unique set of skills as easily."

"I get what you're saying. I don't like it—but I understand."

"Don't tell Simon," Vic said. "I will. I swear. Just—not yet. I need to work out the details first."

Ross scowled. "Okay. Just don't let it get too far. Simon loves you. He deserves the truth."

"He deserves everything," Vic replied. "Don't worry—I'm not going to fuck this up."

"Humph. That remains to be seen."

When they went into the station, Vic found a storage box on his desk and saw that the ticket was gone and an evidence receipt was in its place. "Wow. They turned that around mighty fast. I guess the cold case folks weren't busy today," he said, reading the list of contents. "Looks like all the files. They must not have bothered digitizing that far back."

Ross went to get coffee for them while Vic logged into his Springsteen fan accounts. He spent the next hour chiming in on conversations, pretending to be excited about an upcoming concert. When Vic signed off, he felt a mixture of triumph and nausea. Putting himself in the crosshairs might be for a good cause, but it sent an alarm through all his well-honed defensive instincts.

"If you're done painting a target on your back, let's see what's in the box," Ross said, setting two steaming cups down on their desks.

"Let's split up the focus. How about if you track down the law enforcement involvement? See if anyone who worked the case is still alive and how to get in contact. Maybe there's something they didn't put in the notes."

"That's a long shot after all this time," Ross warned. "If they were older than rookies, they'll be in their eighties by now. They might not remember the case at all, let alone the details."

"Worth a try," Vic replied. "I'm going to go over the victim files and see if there's anything Walt missed. He's a good reporter, but he's working from different source material. There might be something he overlooked."

"Unless the cops at the time didn't bother taking down any information at all," Ross pointed out.

"God, you're such an optimist."

As the end of the day rolled around, Vic's vision blurred from the yellowed pages, bad typing, and lousy handwriting of detectives from a prior generation. He set down his file, blinked, and squeezed his eyes closed, then gave up and rubbed them. "All cops should be required to take penmanship classes," he groused. "Their side notes are chicken scratch. Small, blurry, faded chicken scratch."

"Pick up on anything else?" Ross rubbed his temples which was a sure sign he had a headache.

"There's not much more than the original intake form for most of these." Vic's disgust for the laziness of the cops at the time was clear in his voice. "But on a couple of the reports, someone actually bothered to go beyond the basics. They didn't make a big effort, but they at least did more than fill out the paperwork."

"Anything useful?"

Vic sat back in his chair and stretched. "All young women who worked hospitality jobs. They didn't work at the same hotels or restaurants, and many of the places aren't around anymore. Some are—and since those are family-owned, we might find someone who remembers."

He sighed. "I've got a gut impression that the hospitality piece is important. I mean, it makes sense. They probably had late shifts, coming home alone, living in cheap apartments that catered to people who didn't stick around. They weren't from here, so they didn't come back to the family house where someone would notice right away if they were late."

"Odds are that they knew the killer—at least tangentially," Ross speculated. "Security guard, night clerk at the 24-hour diner, taxi driver."

"They didn't live in the same place, so it's not a doorman or desk clerk," Vic mused.

"And if they worked in different places, it's not a creepy co-worker. Now we've got to look for points of intersection. What did they all do?"

Vic glanced at his watch. "I haven't figured that out yet, but it's going to wait until tomorrow. It's my turn to pick up dinner."

They packed up the box and secured it in Hargrove's office. To Vic's relief, the reporters had given up, and they didn't have to maneuver past a crush of people waving microphones and sticking cameras in their faces.

Vic had ordered dinner online before leaving the precinct house. Picking up Chinese food from their favorite place guaranteed a good start to the evening, and he added extras he knew Simon liked but often didn't request.

I am not bribing him. Oh, what the fuck am I saying. I am totally planning to ply him with food, wine, and sex and then tell him I'm playing bait for a psychopath. I'm going to be sleeping on the couch for a month.

Maybe if I pick up flowers…

He arrived at the blue bungalow with shrimp fried rice, Hunan beef, scallion chicken, hot and sour soup, egg rolls, and Crab Rangoon. The weather had turned colder—a relative statement given that Myrtle Beach's winters were often the same temperature as Pittsburgh's summers.

Vic bought a bouquet of brightly colored flowers from the grocery store, a mix of pretty blooms that he knew Simon would enjoy. While he was there, he also picked up a Key Lime pie, one of Simon's favorites.

I am so screwed.

4

SIMON

Simon felt too jittery to go back to the store after he left the police department. A phone call assured him that Pete was fine and that the reporters were keeping their distance. That helped Simon decide to take a detour and hope his instincts proved right.

He stopped at The Golden Strand, one of the locations where a victim of the eighties killer had worked. He didn't know if Michelle worked bar this afternoon, but he felt a strong nudge to stop in.

"Hiya, Simon," Michelle greeted him from the nearly-empty bar. She shot him a broad grin and waved him over.

"It's been a busy few months," Simon said, an extreme understatement. "You look like life's been good to you."

Michelle's skin glowed, her long dark hair had a healthy shine, and she no longer looked dangerously thin. Simon had known her since she'd come to Myrtle Beach while she was transitioning a few years ago, looking for a place to start over where no one would deadname her and she could reinvent herself. That plan seemed to be working well.

"It has," Michelle agreed. "It took a while like you kept telling me it would, but…now it's real good. And thanks to you, I no longer have to listen to everyone's rambling thoughts."

Michelle was a natural telepath, but like so many of Simon's "Skeleton Crew," no one had recognized, appreciated, or nurtured her gift. Native psychic abilities too often were misunderstood as mental illness, especially when they involved hearing voices or seeing things that weren't there. The mainstream had a long way to go when it came to accepting different ways of knowing or perceiving.

"Glad to help. So the shielding is working?" Simon had taught Michelle how to block the intrusive thoughts of people around her, making it possible for her to tune in only when she wanted so she—and they—could have privacy and boundaries.

"Most of the time. Some people think really loudly, you know?"

Simon chuckled. "Oh, I understand. I pick up on it differently, but I get what you mean. My fiancé can be one of those folks when he's upset."

"Yeah?" She brought Simon a club soda with lime and waved him off when he tried to pay. "On me. You're a cheap date—and I figured you'd want soda since it's during the day." She paused. "Can I ask you something?"

"Sure."

Michelle bit her lip. "I've been seeing someone. Finally got up the nerve. Kelli and I have been going out for a few months, and it's getting serious. But it's hard to be with someone and stay out of their head. I try—I don't want to pry, and reading thoughts is worse than going through someone's phone. But sometimes what she's thinking just blurts out, especially if we're, um—"

"High emotions make it difficult to block," Simon commiserated, saving Michelle the need to finish her sentence; he didn't need to be psychic to know from her blush what she meant.

"Right. Kelli's trying to understand, but it's not the usual dating issue. So how do you handle it?"

"Wow. No one ever asked me that before." Simon took a sip of his drink and thought for a moment. "Remember—my gift works differently than yours. I get images instead of thoughts, usually in bits and pieces and not the whole story. So it's not the same as accidentally listening in to a mental conversation."

"They don't really write books about this stuff." Michelle went down the bar to take another order and returned after a few minutes.

That gave Simon time to ponder. "Maybe there's a different way to think about it," he said when she came back. "When you're with someone in close quarters for a while, you start to finish each other's sentences and guess what they're going to say before they say it. In a way, it's a private language."

Michelle gave him a wistful smile. "I don't have a lot of experience with that kind of relationship, but I follow what you're saying—theoretically, at least."

"Maybe when it comes to being with a long-term partner, it's something you both learn to embrace. Yes, it gives you something of an unfair advantage—but you can choose not to pay attention even if you can't help hearing something going on."

She frowned. "I'm working on that. But—yes."

"I'm betting over time Kelli will figure out tricks—like humming while she thinks or blanking her mind. Kind of like going 'la-la-la.' And you'll learn how to tune out."

"So you're saying to go with the flow instead of fighting it?"

Simon shrugged. "Basically."

Michelle was silent for a moment and then nodded. "Okay. Which probably means that if she's the right one for me, she'll be able to deal with it, and if she isn't, she won't."

Simon smiled. "Yeah. Believe me—Vic and I were poles apart at the beginning. He didn't want to believe my abilities were real. Then we went through some stuff, and it got better. Now—we work around it."

Michelle covered his hand for a moment. "Thank you. That means a lot." She went to serve a guy a beer and returned. "Now—you didn't come here to solve my personal problems." Her eyes went wide. "Did you?"

"I didn't get a vision about your love connection issues." Simon chuckled. "I wanted to ask if anyone at The Strand has been around since the eighties."

Her eyes narrowed. Simon felt a light pressure against his shielding, but his protections held.

"Hey, I had to try," Michelle said. "You're good practice. Maybe someday I'll have walls like that. So—why do you want to know?"

"A young woman who worked as a server here went missing and was never found. Lisa Murdock. I know it's a long time ago, but I think it's somehow connected to something more recent."

He could almost guess Michelle's thoughts. She had helped with tips when he and Vic pursued the Slitter, so he knew she'd make the connections.

"Work here long enough, and you hear the story of the girl who disappeared," Michelle said. "It's break room gossip—almost an urban legend. I wasn't sure she was real until you said something. I thought it was one of those cautionary tales to warn us to be careful going home late at night."

"What's the story?" Simon knew that after all this time, the details could have changed with the telling.

"Just that she worked her shift, got on the shuttle home, and was never seen again," Michelle replied.

"The shuttle?"

Michelle shrugged. "Back in the day, the hotels ran a shuttle at the end of each shift. Myrtle Beach didn't have much in the way of busses back then, taxis were too expensive, a lot of workers couldn't afford cars, and there weren't ride shares."

"So the shuttle went to multiple hotels?"

"From what I hear, it covered hotels, bars, and restaurants."

"So a driver might pick up people at more than one stop?" Simon felt his heart pound as he realized what Michelle's comment meant.

"Yeah. At least, that's what the stories say."

"Is there anyone still around who remembers those days?" Simon felt he was onto something important.

Michelle thought for a moment. "Leanne in housekeeping has been here since God was a pup. I think she started when she was sixteen. She's in her seventies, and she won't retire."

"Perfect. If she didn't know Lisa, she probably heard the story close to the source."

Michelle grinned. "Oh, I'm sure she heard it. Not much gets past Leanne. She's our resident historian."

"When is she in?"

"Mornings. She's past optional retirement age, but she says that she wouldn't know what to do with herself if she didn't work, and since she's management now instead of making beds, it's easy on old joints."

"I'll be back in the morning then," Simon told her, draining the last of his club soda. "Thank you. You're amazing!"

"Right back atcha," Michelle said with a mock salute.

Simon set an alarm on his phone with a meeting note, and left the bar, heading for his next stop, Botanica Hernandez.

"Simon. I knew you'd be here—just not sure when. Good to see you." Gabriella Hernandez greeted him as he walked into the shop. The smell of sage and marigold was a heady mixture, and all of Simon's psychic senses sparked at the energy of the store.

Gabriella stood behind the counter as if she'd just been to the salon. If anything, she looked more like an upscale real estate agent than a powerful bruja. "It's been too long, Simon. Now, tell me what's on your mind."

"You grew up here, right?" Simon gave Gabriella a hug as she came around the counter.

Gabriella gave him a look that Simon sensed down to his bones.

"Yes. Let's go elsewhere to talk." She spoke to a helper in rapid Spanish to take over the front while leading Simon to the break room in the back.

Gabriella made him hot chocolate spiced with cayenne and brought out a plate of cookies which they ate as Simon caught her up on what was going on.

"What do you need?" she asked.

Simon told her the whole story, including Walt's theory of a second-but-unrecognized serial killer and the connection to the current Slitter trial.

Gabriella shook her head and muttered something under her breath in Spanish. "Boy, when you step in shit, it's ankle-deep."

"It's a talent."

"I'd say that it's a curse, but that's no laughing matter," Gabriella replied. "*Mijo*. So much loss—how can you bear it?" She shook her head and touched her protective medallion that hung from a chain around her throat.

Simon shrugged. "It is what it is."

"What do you need?" Gabriella asked.

"Protection hexes, spells, and amulets. I believe that a super-fan of the Slitter is out for blood, and Vic and I are on his list," Simon confessed. "Beyond that, discernment magic. I've got to figure out who is sending dangerously hexed objects to people and break those curses."

"You don't do anything by halves, do you?" Gabriella made the sign of the cross. She muttered something under her breath that Simon didn't quite catch, perhaps a prayer or incantation.

"Apparently not," Simon replied with a sheepish smile.

Gabriella was quiet while she sipped her drink. "Many of the people who work in hospitality jobs are Latinos—that's been true for a long time. Are any of your missing people from our community? Give me their names and I will ask around. People who might not talk to you will confide in me."

Simon checked his list and wrote out the names that he thought might be a fit. "Thank you. This won't bring the lost ones back, but it might give the families closure."

"Don't hope for much—a lot of folks just pass through a town like this on their way to somewhere else," Gabriella warned him. "I might hit a dead end."

Simon smiled. "Thank you for trying."

Gabriella rose and rinsed out her cup. "I have no patience with people who prey on the vulnerable." She gave Simon a shrewd look. "It seems to me you're working three cases at once. The Slitter, the old disappearances, and whoever is sending the cursed objects. That last person is dangerous. They haven't killed—yet. But I believe they are capable of doing so."

"That's what I'm afraid of, too."

"Come with me."

Simon followed Gabriella into the botanica. He dogged her steps as she moved about the shop selecting items to fill a basket—some of which he recognized, and others that were a mystery. He trusted Gabriella to explain eventually.

She returned to the kitchen with a full basket and gestured for Simon to sit across from her.

"Now, we will make charms and hex bags—and I will give you the spells you asked for."

"Do you know what kind of magic is used to connect the cursed objects to the recipient and link the long-ago misfortune to now? I've heard of 'sympathetic magic,' but never something quite this elaborate."

Gabriella was quiet for a moment. "It is a matter of scale and power, but you have the essence of the concept. Like calls to like. There are two types of this magic—I think of them as being 'forward' and 'back.' With the backward magic, what is done to an object affects the person who once owned the item. So to burn a person, the witch would set a lock of hair on fire."

Simon nodded. "That's the principle behind 'Voodoo dolls,' right?"

Gabriella made a face. "Bastardized by Hollywood, but yes." She drummed her fingers on the table as she thought. "What I think of as 'forward' magic is at work in the objects you mentioned. The curse doesn't affect the baseball player—it touches the person who receives his card. The same with the poker chip. It's trickier than the first kind."

"Does it take more skill or just more power?" Simon wasn't a witch, but he knew that even with his type of abilities, the line between native skill and raw power could make a difference.

"Depends on what the goal is," Gabriella said. "For what you've described, some of both I'd wager. My guess is that your 'copycat' might have been an accomplice of the Slitter in some way. Maybe he saw things and didn't report them—which he regards as actively helping. He admires the killer's daring, which he lacks himself."

"You're sure it's a man?"

Another shrug. "Women tend to kill for personal reasons. Men kill for sport. There are exceptions, of course. But my sense is that holds true in this."

"I'd side with your 'sense,'" Simon replied with a smile.

"You're a good boy." As she talked, Gabriella made hex bags, mixing dried leaves, small bones, gemstones, and other magical oddments. She tied the tiny burlap bags off with yarn that Simon could tell—even at a distance—had magic spun into it.

"These will fend off malicious magic, but they have a limited range," she explained. "Carry them on your person. Their effectiveness wanes with distance."

"Okay. What else?"

She took a block of wax and put it in a warmer, standing over it as the heat made it pliable and the light perfume of its scent filled the air, a mix of sandalwood and patchouli. To that, she added a sprinkle of powdered plants known for their protective qualities, including sage, anise, and juniper. The smell relaxed Simon and made him feel safe.

Gabriella murmured an incantation under her breath as she formed the warm wax into cylinders and sank wicks into them.

"You'll need to let these harden, but burning them will amplify the hex bag magic and create a wider area of safety," she told Simon.

Next, Gabriella took a journal from the basket and a fountain pen imbued with magic that Simon could feel even at a distance. "I'm going to write a protection spell, and one for clear-seeing— what you called 'discernment.' The first will amplify positive energy and provide a safe area. The other will cut through illusions—handy if you want to look at an object and see if it's malicious."

"I'm not a witch," Simon reminded Gabriella. "So I hope they're simple."

"Don't underestimate 'simple.' The oldest, most powerful magic is simple at its root. These are created taking your abilities into consideration."

When she finished writing and handed the paper to Simon, he could have sworn the note nearly sparked with energy.

"Keep this on you at all times," Gabriella said as she handed over a silver medallion etched with runes. "You've heard of the Rule of Three?"

Simon nodded. "Whatever energy you send into the world comes back to you three times over."

"The rule also is a warning for those who would use magic to do harm. And while the rule is always effective, it can take time to do its work. This medallion makes the reflection more immediate." She met his gaze. "Clasp the medal in your hand and will your intention. This will send what is directed at you back to its source."

"The charms will keep you and a few friends *safer,* but they can't protect you from everything," Gabriella warned. "The spells should serve your purpose. Be careful, Simon. Old evil and dark magics do not give way easily."

Simon thanked her and paid for the items. "Keep an ear out, please, in case you hear anything related to the cases. It's a long shot, but—"

Gabriella nodded. "I will check with my sources. Those lost souls deserve to find rest."

Simon found several customers browsing in Grand Strand Ghost Tours when he arrived. He stood back, watching Pete do a great job answering questions and making suggestions. Pete had gained a lot of skill and confidence since he started working at the store, and his costumed and theatrical ghost tours were popular with tourists who wanted something a bit more "lively" than Simon's own historical presentations.

He went into the office and left the bag from the botanica on his desk while Pete finished ringing up the purchases. Simon came out carrying a cup of coffee for each of them, and Pete groaned in exaggerated bliss when he took the mug and cradled it between his hands.

"Bless you. Every time I headed for the kitchen, someone came in. I know that's a good problem to have, but I'm caffeine deprived!"

Simon gave Pete a short recap of what he'd learned. "Did I miss anything here?"

Pete took another sip of coffee. "Your reporter friend showed up. Walt. He didn't come inside, but the wards didn't keep him away from the door like it did the others."

Simon frowned. He'd need to think about what that meant since the wards didn't consider Walt to be a threat. "What did he want?"

Pete set his mug aside. "I went out to him since he gestured through the window that he wanted to tell me something." He rolled his eyes. "I was sorta afraid he might break into interpretive dance."

"It's the boardwalk. No one would notice."

"You might be right about that," Pete replied with a grin. "But I spared us all finding out. When Walt realized you weren't here, he gave me this for you." Pete handed Simon a folded piece of paper. "Said you should call him if you want details."

Simon unfolded the note and read it aloud. "I found a man who covered the crime beat for the local newspaper when the disappearances happened. He's old but sharp. Might still have his notes from back in the day. If you want to meet him, call me, and I can arrange it." Walt had scrawled his number underneath the message.

"You gonna go see him?"

Simon shook his head. "Not today. I'll call to make an appointment for tomorrow. I need to talk to some dead people first."

"Alrighty then. I'll cover the front, and you chat up the Caspers."

Simon stopped in the kitchen long enough to grab a bottle of water and an energy bar for after his séance. He thought about going up to the small apartment over the shop for privacy but decided that if the effort kicked his ass, he wanted Pete close enough to help. An intense session with spirits could leave Simon drained or unconscious, which was why Vic wanted to make sure Simon wasn't alone when he called the ghosts.

The office energy felt wrong for this kind of working, so Simon closed the door between the shop and the kitchen and settled at the table. He closed his eyes and focused on his breathing, centering himself and opening his gift.

"Hey, Dante—are you there? I need your help." Normally Simon would have called to a spirit more formally, but Dante was his ancestor and showed up on a fairly regular basis. He and Dante had teamed up on several cases, and Simon had used his mediumship to allow Dante to inhabit his body for short periods. Sometimes, the ghost dropped by just to hang out.

Simon waited, unsure exactly where ghosts went in between appearances and how his call traveled between the worlds of the living and dead. When the temperature plummeted in the small kitchen, and Simon felt the hair on his arms stand up, he knew Dante had heard him.

"It's good to see you," Dante said before his apparition became visible. Simon blinked, and suddenly his ancestor stood on the other side of the table, still dressed like the Revolutionary War-era privateer he had once been.

"Good to see you as well," Simon replied. "How are you at finding other ghosts?"

Dante regarded him questioningly. *"If there are spirits nearby, I see them—just as you see people on the street. Even if a ghost tried to hide, I would sense their presence. Why do you ask?"*

Simon explained about the long-ago missing people and having encountered three of their ghosts so far. "No one ever solved their cases," he told Dante. "They deserve that much, even if the one who hurt them is already dead."

Dante nodded solemnly. *"I agree. How can I help?"*

Simon spread his hands in a shrug. "I'm not completely sure because I don't really know how the whole ghost thing works. But if you stick around Myrtle Beach, can you please keep an eye out for the ghosts of young women who seem unsettled? I'm trying to reach the ones on my list, but there may be others no one knew about. Or some of the ghosts may be afraid to come to me, but they might talk to you."

Dante laughed. *"I'll try. It depends on how much of themselves they remember. Some spirits fade over time if they don't know how to move on and have no purpose for staying. Do you know more about these young women? Clearly you believe they came to a bad end."*

Simon didn't want Dante near his laptop since ghosts could cause problems with electronics. He had printed out the photos of the missing women and pushed those printouts across the table to where Dante stood. The ghost studied the images intently.

"Where might their spirits roam?" Dante's archaic phrasing always made Simon smile.

"They all worked at hotels and restaurants downtown, but I don't think they were killed there. Too public. I found out that they took a…shared carriage…to get to work. Maybe they haunt the station."

Dante looked thoughtful. *"If you will show me where this station is, I will keep an eye out for spirits that might be your missing women. I hope you can give them peace."*

"You and me, both," Simon replied fervently. "Thank you."

Dante grinned and gave a deep bow; then his image dissipated like fog scattered on the breeze. The room's temperature rose, and Simon felt a wave of fatigue wash over him.

Calling Dante didn't take as much energy as searching for spirits Simon didn't know. Then again, talking to people he knew took less effort than meeting strangers, so Simon figured that it made sense for the same to hold true on the ethereal plane.

Simon pulled out the list of names from the same folder and read through them as he fortified himself with water and half a protein bar. He picked the first name, settled into his chair, and closed his eyes.

"Carolyn Hass. If you can hear my voice, find me. I need to talk with you."

Simon waited, trusting the process even if he didn't completely understand how it worked. After a few minutes, the temperature grew colder once more. Unlike Dante, this spirit seemed to be struggling to follow the call to its source, unsure of what to do, or unable to make herself seen and heard.

Carolyn couldn't manifest. Instead, she became an image in Simon's mind, matching the photo on the long-ago police report. Carolyn looked to be in her early twenties, with dark hair pulled up in a ponytail, wearing a housekeeping uniform and sensible shoes for a job that kept her on her feet all day.

"Thank you for answering my call," Simon told the spirit. She seemed nervous, and her image wavered like she was either unsure about how to maintain the connection or lacked the energy.

"Did you run away, or did someone kill you?" Simon asked.

"Killed."

"Did you see your killer?"

Carolyn shook her head. *"Grabbed from behind."*

"Do you know where your body is buried?"

"In the caves."

Simon leaned forward. "What caves, Carolyn? Where are the caves?"

The image flickered wildly. *"Near the ocean. And the castle. No surrender."*

"Castle?"

Carolyn opened her mouth to speak, but Simon couldn't hear her words. Then abruptly, the ghost vanished.

"Caves near the ocean and a castle?" Simon repeated, confused. Carolyn's spirit was gone, so getting a follow-up answer didn't look likely, at least for today. He felt a headache coming on, which meant his ghost whispering was over for today.

Simon knew Vic would be cross if he pushed himself hard enough to pass out, and he had no desire to face his partner's disapproval or the worse-than-a-hangover morning-after that went with overextending his gift.

Instead, he turned to the internet, searching every mention he could find for "caves" and "castle" in the vicinity of Myrtle Beach.

The only castle near the Grand Strand was the Atalaya, a 1930s mansion that had fallen into ruin. Locals often referred to it as Atalaya Castle, even though it was long past its glory days.

Simon paged through the online photos of Atalaya. Nothing about the site pinged his intuition or made it a likely dumping ground for a murderer. It was too far from the main stretch of hotels and restaurants where the missing women worked and not easy to get into or out of for someone with a struggling kidnap victim or a body to hide.

The other search results for caves or castles referred to elaborate mini-golf courses or random businesses built long after Carolyn and the others disappeared. If the other spirit hadn't told him about the caves, Simon would have wondered whether he had heard correctly or if the ghost had gotten confused.

Which meant he needed to figure out what someone in 1982 might have meant by those words, even if time had changed the landscape.

Tomorrow morning, I'll go back to The Strand and see if the woman Michelle mentioned will see me. Maybe she'll remember something about the missing people or the "caves" that will put us on the right track.

Carolyn's last comment stuck in Simon's mind. *What did she mean about "surrender"? Surrendering to her killer? To death?*

The drain of calling to Dante and Carolyn hit, and Simon could barely keep his eyes open. After finishing his snack to replenish his energy and checking on Pete, Simon begged off for half an hour to nap.

He fell asleep almost immediately, and the dreams closed in. *Simon found himself running through a dark forest, pursued by something he couldn't see. His pounding footsteps and the rasp of his breath drowned out any other sounds. He knew that whatever chased him was on his heels, and he couldn't keep up this pace forever.*

Just as quickly, the forest vanished, and Simon was in bed, unable to move or cry out. He wanted to struggle and shout for help, but his body refused to obey, and no one heard his screams.

Shadows ringed the cold, dark room in his vision. Simon struggled to breathe as if the darkness pulled the air from his lungs and the warmth from his body. He shuddered in fear, knowing that something lurked unseen in the corners.

"Hey, boss. Simon. Wake up!" Pete's voice cut through the terror, and Simon clung to it like a life rope, following it back to the light. He found himself unharmed on the couch in his office, panting for breath as if he'd nearly been smothered, shivering although the room was comfortably warm.

"What—?" Simon felt groggy, almost drugged.

"I heard you thrashing and crying out and figured I'd better come to the rescue," Pete replied, and Simon eyed the pitcher of water in one hand, can of soda in the other. "If worst came to worst, I figured I'd douse you and see if it woke you up. Fortunately, it didn't come to that."

"Fortunately," Simon agreed, still not quite himself.

"Vision? Nightmare?"

Simon shook his head, happy for the can of soda Pete pressed into his hand. He glugged it down, waiting for the sugar to hit his system. Gradually, Simon felt his energy return and his thoughts clear.

"I'm not sure—more of a memory, but not mine. I'm wondering if the spirit who came to me found another way to communicate. I think she was trying to tell me something that she couldn't put into words. It felt like a psychic attack."

Pete frowned. "I thought the shop was warded so that kind of thing couldn't happen."

"It can't," Simon replied. "That's why I think it's someone else's memory. Carolyn showed me something she wasn't able to tell me."

"Carolyn? Who's Carolyn? Anyway, how does that fit in with a serial killer who got away with murder?" Pete asked the question that Simon had been wondering.

"Carolyn was one of the missing women. As for the other part, I don't know yet," he admitted. "I don't understand what about the Slitter's case has upset the ghosts from the eighties killer or where the 'fanboy' sending the cursed objects comes in. I can't shake the feeling that it all goes together, but I can't see the whole picture yet."

Despite the upsetting vision, Simon insisted on working in the shop for the rest of the day. He knew Vic would probably be late, and he didn't want to be alone. If Pete suspected that Simon's jitters kept him from leaving early, he didn't mention it.

Fortunately, the late afternoon proved busy, keeping Simon's mind off worrisome questions. His mood improved as he booked tour guests, helped customers choose merchandise, and answered questions about the books he'd written on local ghosts and hauntings.

He glanced at his phone when a message notice hit his inbox from one of the venues he had emailed for estimates on wedding receptions. Simon smiled, reading down through the friendly and informative note, then thumbed through the photos.

"You're looking smitten. Get an email from Vic?" Pete teased.

Simon shook his head. "No—just some preliminary research on wedding venues and places for a reception."

"Have you set a date?"

"Nah—you'd be among the first to know if we had. I'm coming at it a little backward, I guess. Once we find the place we want, their openings will determine our choice of dates."

"You thinking big and splashy or small and intimate?" Pete asked, leaning against the counter. They were nearly at closing time, and the shop was empty for the first time in hours.

"Intimate, but maybe not small given the size of Vic's extended family," Simon said with a chuckle. "I've looked at a lot of the hotels. They have gorgeous ocean views, and I'm sure the food would be great, but they're hella expensive. And I don't want to risk planning everything to be outdoors—you know how the weather can change here at the drop of a hat."

Simon opened the photos he had just received and handed Pete his phone. "I looked at the Train Depot on a whim, but now I'm intrigued. I think it's big enough for his family and our friends. They have relationships with caterers and DJs. It's not a religious site—which avoids some problems—and as far as I can tell, there's nothing problematic about it historically, which is hard to find in the South."

"Is it haunted?"

"No—another point in its favor, although neither are most of the hotels," Simon replied. "I've got to admit; I like that it's quirky. From the photos, they put on a really nice event with twinkle lights and centerpieces and a dance floor. And it's definitely more affordable."

"No ocean view," Pete pointed out.

Simon gestured toward the shop's large front windows. "Dude,

I've got an ocean view all day, every day. We can always do our photos on the beach, weather permitting."

"That could be really nice." Pete handed back Simon's phone. "Memorable and unique. I've been to some wedding receptions in the hotels. They do good events, but they're rather…cookie cutter. Slick. The Train Depot would be pretty cool."

Simon slipped his phone back into his pocket. "Thanks. I haven't run it by Vic yet. Like I said—preliminary research." He twisted the ring on his right hand, still feeling the thrill of the promise they had made to each other. Even though they hadn't chosen a date, looking at venues and figuring out all the other pieces —cakes, photographers, music, and more—made it feel real.

Simon and Pete closed up together, and Simon walked Pete to his car.

"The reporters stayed clear today," Pete observed. "Maybe they've found somewhere more interesting."

Simon appreciated Pete's optimism. "I'm waiting for the other shoe to drop. They'll be back."

Simon saw Pete off and headed home, relieved when he saw that reporters weren't camped outside the blue bungalow.

Once he was inside, he checked his phone for missed messages. The rest of his Skeleton Crew hadn't turned up any information about caves, but Gabriella was able to talk to the families of the victims on the list. Their stories corroborated what Simon had already learned, which was helpful but didn't add new insights.

His phone vibrated, and Simon saw a text from Vic letting him know he'd be running late but that he hadn't forgotten about picking up dinner.

Simon: *Just be careful,* Simon texted back. *Come home safe.*

5

VIC

"Sorry I'm late. But the food is hot." Vic hurried into the house, set the take-out bags on the table, and handed off the bouquet to Simon, then grabbed him by the belt loops and pulled him in for a kiss. "Miss me?"

"Always," Simon replied when he came up for air.

Vic set out the Chinese food on the table. Simon stopped to sniff the flowers as he put them in a vase, closing his eyes and smiling wide. Vic loved to see Simon smile, and if bringing home some blooms would make those dimples pop, Vic vowed to do that more often.

"Eat first, then talk shop." Vic chuckled as Simon's stomach growled.

He knew that cops tended to have a hard time leaving work at the office. Coming from a law enforcement family, Vic understood the dangers of the job—physical, psychological, and the toll taken on relationships.

Having Simon as his official partner on cases with a supernatural angle helped, but sometimes that meant that they both had trouble separating personal time from work. Feeling guilty for taking time off with an unsolved crime in the balance didn't help.

They talked about everything except the case while they ate. Vic had intentionally scrolled through headlines to have conversation topics since his day had focused on nothing but the Slitter investigation and the attacks on the D.A. and the judge—and waiting for the fanboy to take the bait. Vic had the feeling that Simon was holding back as well. That worried him and made him wonder what Simon had discovered and just how much he had dug into old unsolved cases.

"What do you think about the old Train Depot?" Simon blurted when they were about halfway through the meal.

Vic blinked, completely confused. "The old depot? I don't have any thoughts about it. Should I? Did something happen there?"

"Our wedding—maybe?"

Vic managed a bemused smile. "I think you had half of that conversation in your head without me. Want to start from the beginning—out loud this time?"

Simon looked chagrined. "Sorry. Bad habit."

Vic reached out to take his hand. "No apologies necessary—I just feel like I'm coming in on the middle of the discussion. Now, what was that about our wedding?"

Simon blushed. "I've been looking at places to have the reception—and maybe the ceremony as well. It's fun to do and breaks up the day. The hotels around here are pretty but expensive, and they all look the same. But the old train depot was made over into an event venue, and it has a lot of character."

"I can't say I've ever paid any attention to it, but maybe you and I can go over and have a look," Vic offered. "It sounds interesting. Anything we do will break the D'Amato wedding mold since High Church Catholic Mass is out."

"It's probably going to depend on how many of your clan are planning to come and whether there's room, as much as it does on price," Simon replied. "Do you have an idea based on the other weddings?"

Vic leaned back in his chair, still holding Simon's hand. He loved the idea of Simon doing some wedding planning on the side, even if they hadn't set a date. While Vic occasionally got panicked about tying the knot, he knew he wanted to spend the rest of his life with Simon. More often, he had flashes of doubt about whether Simon would decide he could do better. So finding out that his fiancé was so invested in the wedding reassured Vic's unspoken insecurities.

"If we were getting hitched in Pittsburgh, we'd get the whole extended family," Vic replied. "My cousin had four hundred at her wedding, and most of that was on our side."

Simon paled. "Four *hundred*? Dude—I don't think I'm *related* to four hundred people—including the ghosts."

Vic laughed. "Don't panic—a lot of those folks won't caravan all the way down here for little ol' me." He paused to do the math in his head, counting siblings, first cousins, aunts, and uncles. "I'd bet one hundred to one hundred fifty, tops."

"Okay," Simon said, looking like he might hyperventilate. "We'll have room since I'm not inviting my family. But I do want to invite our friends. Tracey and Shayna, Pete and Mikki, Ross and Sheila, Gabriella, Miss Eppie, Captain Hargrove…and then there's Cassidy and the Charleston crew. And I figured we'd invite Travis and Brent, Seth and Evan, as well as Erik and Ben—I know it's farther for them, but it would be great if they could make it."

"Hmm. Are you including Sorren? Because if so, we need an evening event," Vic pointed out. Sorren was a nearly six-hundred-year-old vampire who worked closely with Simon's cousin Cassidy to help stop supernatural threats. He and Simon had been part of a few of those efforts and had gotten to know Cassidy's friends and allies.

"I assumed so," Simon replied. "And I wouldn't be surprised if he showed up."

"Just as well we aren't doing a Mass then."

"Probably so."

Vic realized he'd come a long way from doubting that psychics were real to inviting a vampire to his wedding.

"Go ahead and make an appointment or whatever we have to do to go see the place. We can figure it out from there," Vic said.

Simon leaned over the table to press a kiss to Vic's lips. "Thank you. I'm glad you didn't mind me doing some research—I wasn't trying to leave you out of anything."

Vic cupped the back of Simon's head and deepened the kiss for a moment before releasing him. "I'm just grateful you're having fun doing it. One of us needs to—and I've been too slammed with work to think about anything else."

"Let's get the kitchen cleaned up, and then I've got some tidbits that might be useful," Simon told him.

Once the dishes were done and the leftovers put away, Simon and Vic settled onto the couch with a couple of beers. Vic listened as Simon recounted his day, then filled him in on what he and Ross had uncovered.

"Caves and a castle? That's some freaky shit." Vic took a pull from his beer. "And what do you think 'no surrender' means?"

"I'm still not sure about that, although I've got my theories. I'm hoping that either the woman at The Strand or the retired reporter Walt knows can shed some light on things," Simon admitted. He reached for a bag and pulled out the items Gabriella had made for him.

"These are for you, Ross, and Hargrove," he said, handing Vic three of the hex bags. "Keep them with you at all times. It's kind of like Kevlar for magic."

"Okay." Vic drew out the word. Maybe he imagined it, but he could have sworn he felt a ripple of energy when he touched the burlap. "After all the stuff that's happened, I don't think Ross and Hargrove will bat an eye at this. Do I want to know how it works?"

"They concentrate protective energy. If you want specifics, you'll have to talk to Gabriella. I believe her when she says they'll keep you safer—but they won't make you bulletproof."

"Got it," Vic said. "Thank you."

"You're welcome. You're my partner—of course I want to keep you safe." Simon paused. "You have other amulets. Please wear them while we're dealing with this."

Vic could see how much it meant to Simon. "I promise." He leaned back and closed his eyes. "I'm honestly afraid the Slitter trial might run into complications, Simon. Things aren't going well."

NO SURRENDER | 87

"Talk to me. Is this about the cursed items?"

Vic nodded. He didn't open his eyes, but he felt Simon's hand on his thigh, a reassuring weight.

"The news ran a segment about 'bad luck' striking the case with the D.A. and now the judge. It was just clickbait—this time. They didn't know about me and the food poisoning. But if someone else gets hit, three times is a definite pattern. The media will go nuts with that kind of thing. It'll turn into a circus—and that's prime territory for a mistrial."

"Do you think it would come to that?" Simon sounded like he'd been sucker-punched.

Vic shrugged. "Maybe. It also creates pressure on the police to figure out who is sending the objects, and we look bad if it takes us too long. Reporters will explain away the danger as coincidence, but the idea that there's a psycho out there sending weird-ass stuff to key players of the trial is something they'll latch onto."

"Any leads?"

"We're going to talk to one of the detectives who handled the eighties disappearances. I wouldn't doubt that he knows the reporter Walt is going to fix you up with," Vic added.

"Walt is hardly 'fixing me up' with anyone."

"You know what I meant." Vic sighed. He sat up and met Simon's gaze. "And you're probably going to kick my ass, but I figured that since our fanboy doesn't know that the ticket made me sick, maybe I could goad him into trying again—and tipping his hand. So I went out to the old Springsteen concert groups I joined a long time ago and raved about the *awesome* vintage ticket someone sent me. We turned the IT guys loose on it like with Andrews's and the Judge's groups to see if we can get a shortlist of suspects. They're already watching the activity and noting likely suspects."

Simon glared at him. "You're setting yourself up as bait. I hate that."

"This time, I know not to touch anything unusual."

"Cursed objects can kill, Vic. This isn't a game."

Simon was pissed, but underneath the anger, Vic knew his

partner was afraid. He reached out and took Simon's hands, holding on even when Simon tried to jerk away.

"I know it's not a game. I have every intention of growing old with you. But I'm a cop—and that's a dangerous job. Drawing out a suspect is part of the process. If the IT guys find a match in two fan groups, it could be coincidence. But if they find the same person in three, we have a solid lead that could help us identify the fanboy."

Simon relaxed and didn't try to pull away, but his expression made it clear he still didn't like the plan. "Don't do anything stupid," he grumbled.

"That's asking a lot," Vic teased and saw the corner of Simon's lips twitch. "But I will do everything I can to stay safe. That goes both ways, you know. I'm not the only one who has a history of running into danger."

"Okay," Simon relented. "Is that why you've been stressed all evening?"

"Partly. All the stuff with the reporters gets on my last nerve. It doesn't help that Ross has been edgy. He's not sleeping well. Bad dreams. Can't say I blame him."

"Tell me about Ross's bad dreams." The intensity in Simon's eyes made Vic frown.

"You think it's important?'

"It might be. That vision I had at the shop, I think it was some-thing the girl's ghost experienced."

"Before she died? Like a premonition?"

Simon grimaced. "Not exactly. It didn't foretell her death. More like a private horror movie designed to produce fear and dread. I'm wondering if something supernatural might be behind it."

"A witch? But that's too long ago for the fanboy who's sending the cursed objects, isn't it?"

Simon shook his head. "I think we might have another player on the board—some kind of supernatural entity. Not human."

Vic groaned. "Like we need another loose end? What do you mean—entity?"

"Don't know yet. I need to look into it and tap what Teag and Travis know. I could be wrong."

Vic sat bolt upright, eyes wide. "Maybe not. When Ross and I read over the files from the eighties disappearances, nightmares got mentioned a couple of times. I didn't pay attention to it because with people disappearing, who wouldn't have bad dreams? But that's something to ask the retired detective about."

Simon nodded. "I can mention it to the reporter too. And it's something I'll ask the ghosts if I can find more of them—and our contact at the hotel. It might be nothing—or it could be important."

"If something caused nightmares back in the eighties, why did it hang around until now?" Vic asked.

"I'm not sure," Simon replied, voice fading as he appeared lost in thought about the question. "It could be a person, as you suggested. If it's an entity…creature…it might be immortal or near enough. And the dreams might be what feeds it."

Vic gave Simon a long look. "Please swear you aren't pulling my leg."

"Wish I were, but I'm dead serious—no pun intended."

Vic winced. "Not funny. Are you talking 'feed' like a vampire?"

Simon shrugged. "Yes—and no. There are beings that can feed in other ways than taking blood. They can feed off energy, memories, and fear."

"Shit."

"Yeah, that was my thought."

"Do you think either the Slitter or the fanboy called this…entity?" Vic asked.

Simon paused. "Not necessarily. No one has to call vultures to roadkill. They can smell it. It could be that if enough people are in extreme psychic distress, it's like ringing a dinner bell."

"Awesome," Vic replied sarcastically. "Can they drain someone dry—or kill?"

"Depends on what the entity or creature is," Simon answered. "I need to do some research, and I also need more information about how people are being affected. If I'm right, I'd bet that the judge and the D.A. also had extremely weird dreams—more like night terrors."

Vic looked up as a question occurred to him. "If Ross has been targeted by this entity-creature, why haven't I?"

Simon gestured around them. "Wardings. As long as you sleep here in the bungalow, there are strong spells and protections all around us to keep out exactly that sort of thing. I wouldn't advise taking a catnap at the station—or anywhere else. The hex bag might protect you—but then again, it might not."

Vic scowled. "Hunting a killer is something I know how to do. This other stuff…I'm out of my depth."

Simon took Vic's hands in his. "Good thing you're not alone, huh?" He rubbed his thumbs over Vic's palms. "How about we give all this shop talk a rest for tonight? Let's take a hot shower, blow off some steam," he added with a suggestive grin, "and I'll give you a back rub. I'm pretty sure I can take your mind off work."

Vic gave a low chuckle. "Oh, I don't doubt that."

Vic let the shower warm up while he drew Simon into a kiss. Sometimes their lovemaking was hungry and fast, but tonight they moved slow, savoring each touch. Vic knew they were both weary and worried. This connection was as much about reassurance as it was slaking their thirst.

"Love you," Simon told him as they undressed each other, taking their time.

Vic brushed his fingertips down Simon's cheek, then across his lips. "Love you too. Please, Simon, be careful. There are layers to this situation, and we don't know all the players. Stay safe."

"Same for you," Simon murmured. "I know it's your job. But we're partners—in everything. So please, don't shut me out to try to protect me." He turned and backed into the shower, pulling Vic with him.

Vic ran his hand through Simon's chestnut hair as the water poured over them. "We'll hunt this one together," he promised. "No secrets. Don't take crazy chances." Vic slid his palms down Simon's soap-slick skin, memorizing the feel.

His hand paused over the scar from a bullet wound that had nearly claimed Simon during the Slitter case. Simon's touch faltered over the lookalike scar where a stalker from Vic's past had shot him.

"This is why we both have to be careful." Vic took Simon's hands in his own and held them over his heart. "I can't lose you. You can't lose me. So we have to fight this smart, okay? Promise me."

Simon nodded, and Vic could read the raw emotion in his eyes. "I promise. But that goes both ways."

"I promise." Vic cupped the back of Simon's head with one hand and reached down to squeeze his ass with the other. "Let me seal that with a kiss."

Vic turned so that Simon's back was to the water and sank to his knees, sheltered from the shower spray. He took Simon's half-hard cock in his mouth down to the root, nuzzling the wiry hair at the base. Vic let his tongue swirl over the head and sucked. Simon's prick plumped quickly as Vic's hand slipped between his legs and rolled his balls, then traced his hole with a fingertip.

Simon had one hand on Vic's shoulder and one in his short hair, willing to let Vic set the pace and depth. "God, Vic, feels so good."

Vic hummed in response, loving the shiver that went through Simon's body and the immediate reaction as his stiff cock jumped in Vic's mouth. He palmed a globe of Simon's ass and squeezed, letting a fingertip on the other hand tease the sensitive taint. Vic tasted pre-come and knew Simon was close.

He picked up his pace, licking and sucking until Simon's hips bucked and his body went rigid. Vic swallowed down Simon's release, flicking his tongue to capture the last drops from the now oversensitive knob. He looked up, enjoying the blissed-out expression on Simon's face.

"Relaxed?" Vic smirked.

"Mm-hm." Simon pulled Vic to his feet and turned him, so they stood back to front, then slicked his hand with the lube they kept in the shower and took Vic's hard cock in hand.

"Let me show you *relaxed*," Simon murmured next to Vic's ear. One hand tweaked Vic's nipples as the other pumped his dick in a slow rhythm that gradually picked up speed.

Vic let his head fall back against Simon's shoulder, giving himself up to his lover's touch. "You hit…all the right spots," he managed, knowing that after the day's stress, he wouldn't last long.

"Let go," Simon whispered. "I want to take good care of you."

Vic closed his eyes, wrapped in Simon's arms and engulfed in the shower's steam. He gave himself over completely to the feel of his boyfriend's hand on his cock, slick and tight, building toward release.

He came with a shout, Simon's name on his lips, as his climax barreled through him. For a few seconds, Vic thought he might sag to the floor if Simon hadn't kept him on his feet.

"C'mon. Let's get out of here before we prune." Simon kissed Vic's ear before shifting so that the water sluiced away the jizz, then turned off the shower and handed Vic a towel and took one for himself.

"Don't know about you, but I'm going to sleep just fine after that," Simon said with a chuckle.

Vic let his lover dry him off, then Simon stepped away to towel down before they both pulled on sleep shorts and hurried through getting ready for bed. Once they were under the covers, Vic drew Simon against him, taking comfort from proximity.

"We're going to figure this out," Vic said quietly before he pressed a kiss to Simon's lips.

Simon snuggled closer. "I know we will," he replied, pausing to yawn. "I believe in us."

"...as the trial of William Fischer, the alleged 'Strand Slitter,' draws closer, Grand Strand mental health professionals warn that the publicity around the high-profile murder case has caused a spike in sleep disorders, panic attacks, and night terrors among adults—"

Ross muttered something under his breath and reached for the remote to mute the office TV.

"Hey! I was listening to that," Vic protested.

Ross looked grumpy. "You don't need a reporter to tell you

people can't sleep—including yours truly. The world's going to hell in a handbasket. Not exactly front page, breaking news."

"Simon thinks the sleep disorders might be related."

"To the case? How?"

"Apparently, there are 'entities' that feed off fear, and when bad things happen, they show up like crabs to carrion," Vic replied.

Ross stared at him. "You're serious."

"Unfortunately, yes."

"Shit. So some weird spook is a nightmare voyeur? Now I feel dirty."

Vic checked the time. "Aren't we due to see that retired detective? Better go now if we're going to pick up Krispy Kremes on the way."

"Bribery is illegal."

"Not if it's cops and donuts."

Ross drove. Vic picked up coffee and two dozen "Hot Now" melt-in-your-mouth donuts—one box to eat in the car and the other to sweeten the disposition of the older man they were going to visit.

They pulled up in front of a modest house in a tidy Murrell's Inlet neighborhood. The well-maintained home and yard boded well for the occupant.

"Detective John Gordon?" Vic said when a tall, silver-haired man with craggy features came to the door. "D'Amato and Hamilton—we called ahead to see you. And we brought donuts." Vic flashed his badge while Ross handed over the Krispy Kremes.

"I've been expecting you. Come in." John Gordon moved aside to let them enter.

Vic scanned the room out of habit. His cop senses told him Gordon was widowed, probably for several years. Photos suggested children and grandchildren, with a few of him and a woman Vic guessed had been Gordon's wife. Books and DVDs were neatly shelved, except for a hardcover thriller next to an overstuffed armchair and the case for a classic action movie next to the big screen TV.

"Have a seat. Would you like a soda?"

"No, thank you," Ross declined as he and Vic sat on the couch, and Gordon took his place in the chair.

"Now what's all this about? You mentioned the disappearances back in the eighties. No one wanted to hear about them then. Why now?"

Vic cleared his throat. "We think there might be a connection to the Slitter case. There's a crazy fan stalking people who are involved with the trial, and we're wondering whether Fischer's admirer might have cut his teeth on the unsolved disappearances."

Gordon sat back and looked them over, silent for a moment as he digested Vic's comment. "That's a couple of big leaps of intuition."

Ross nodded. "Yes, sir. We know that."

"What drew your attention to the old cases? Back in the day, the tourism types wanted to bury bad news deeper than the bodies."

Vic grimaced, knowing that the business boosters hated any whiff of scandal. "Walt Baker saw the possible connection. For a reporter, he's a pretty good guy. Ross and I looked into the list of names he gave us and wanted to find out more."

"Huh," Gordon said, shaking his head with a sad smile. "I've met Walt. Paths crossed on a few cases before I retired. Guessing he's still at it? Jimmy Olsen would be proud—talk about a bulldog reporter."

"Guess I shouldn't be surprised the two of you knew each other," Ross said.

"We've read your case reports." Vic leaned forward. "So we know the official take on the situation. But we wondered—was there anything else that you didn't put in the report? Maybe something you figured the powers that be wouldn't have taken seriously?"

Gordon eyed the two men for a long moment. "Like what?"

Vic cleared his throat. "When Ross and I worked the Slitter case, we had another partner—"

"You're the one who works with the psychic," Gordon finished for him, then chuckled when Vic looked surprised.

"I was a detective, remember? I know how to look up someone

who calls me out of the blue to talk about something that happened forty years ago."

"Of course," Vic replied, looking sheepish.

"So what you're really asking is—did I see anything woo-woo? Something ghosty or weird that the bosses wouldn't have believed?"

Ross and Vic nodded. "Or maybe something that hit a little close to the bone," Ross added. "We all know the Strand has its power brokers. Sometimes there's pressure to downplay issues that might be bad for business or could embarrass the wrong people."

"Guess the game hasn't changed much since I've been out of it," Gordon said with a sigh.

"Probably not," Vic agreed.

"Most of the time, I loved my job," Gordon told them. "I felt like I made a difference, that in a small way the world was a better place with each creep we took off the street. One of the things I hated the most were cases where something bad happened to women, and no one believed them."

He was silent for a moment. "That's what got me into policing. My sister was murdered by her boyfriend. At the time, no one on the force wanted to see what was in front of them. They wouldn't investigate and came up with cockamamie excuses why it was her fault she ended up dead."

Even after all this time, Vic could hear the bitterness in the man's voice.

"So I became a homicide detective, and I nailed that son of a bitch's ass to the wall for what he did to Julie," Gordon continued. "There's no statute of limitations on murder."

Vic and Ross exchanged a glance, and Vic's estimation of the older man notched up beyond his impressive record of completed cases.

"I guess that's why I stuck with the cases as long as I could— even after I retired," Gordon confessed. "I had theories, but I couldn't find enough hard evidence to lead to a conviction. In my mind, I had a solid case, but I know how these things go. A good defense attorney could have raised doubts with a jury, and that's all it takes to dismiss a case—and then we'd lose our chance to come after the bastard forever. Only one who seemed to think the same was a reporter following the case, Ed Gallagher. I think he's retired now, too."

"So you had a suspect in mind?" Ross shifted forward with curiosity.

"I'll go to my grave convinced that Eliot Thompson kidnapped those girls—young women—and killed them," Gordon replied. "He had motive, means, and opportunity. Motive—several former girl-friends gave statements that they left him because he liked to 'play rough.' Rough enough to leave scars and break bones."

"Makes sense," Vic said.

"There were also domestic violence calls from his address, but the cases all got dropped. I think his girlfriends were scared of him or got paid off," Gordon went on. "I believe he decided to find new 'playmates' who didn't get to have opinions."

"And no one wanted to follow up?" Vic's fist clenched on the couch beside his hip.

Gordon shrugged. "Not many. Not enough. The way domestic violence calls are handled isn't perfect now, but believe me—it's a damned sight better than it used to be"

"What about means and opportunity? Ross asked.

"Thompson was the main driver for the hospitality worker shuttle that picked up at the hotels and restaurants after hours. Used to call it the 'waitress bus' back in the day. He wasn't the only driver, but he tended to draw the night shift more than other people. Which provided the opportunity—he was someone the riders were familiar with, and he knew where to find vulnerable young women in the wee hours of the morning on their way from the shuttle stop to their apartments."

"And no one questioned him?" Ross's voice clearly showed his frustration.

"Oh, I questioned him several times," Gordon replied. "But he was a smart bastard. Slick. Almost like he was playing cat and mouse with us. All I had was circumstantial evidence. We even searched his apartment, but if he kept trophies from his kills, he didn't hide them there."

"Is he still alive?" Vic sincerely hoped karma had caught up with Thompson, even if the police didn't.

Gordon shook his head. "Thompson had an aggressive type of liver cancer. Killed him within a month of when the last girl went missing. Wonder of all wonders—that's when the disappearances stopped."

Vic knew that he should have been glad that the killing spree had ended, but the victory felt empty since Thompson hadn't been called to account for his crimes.

"Did he have any helpers?" Ross asked. "Were there people you thought ought to have seen something but who either played dumb or might have been an accomplice?"

Gordon nodded and gave a wolfish smile. "Good…you're sharp. Nice to know the younger generation is on the ball."

Vic was thirty-two, and he guessed that Gordon was more than twice his age, so youth was relative.

"Shawna Stinson managed an apartment building popular with service workers because it was cheap and close to the shuttle station. She had a reputation for being a busybody and sticking her nose into her renters' business. But when it came to the women who went missing, she swore she didn't have a clue."

"Yeah, that's not suspicious at all," Ross muttered.

"I know—right?" Gordon replied. "I think she was either scared or paid off, and my bet is the latter."

"She still around?" Vic asked.

Gordon shook his head. "She was older then, and it's been a while. Died about twenty years ago. I don't think she actively set the victims up. But I do believe she knew or suspected who the killer was and refused to help."

"Anyone else?" Vic pressed.

Gordon frowned. "There was a janitor who gave me the creeps. That's very un-scientific, but you seem like good detectives to me, so you'll know what I mean about going with your gut. He split the night shift between the shuttle station and the bus depot. Squirrely little guy, full of questions, always under foot. Maybe he was just bored, but he seemed a little too interested in what we were doing."

"Interested, how?" Ross's eyes narrowed.

"He was just a kid—probably in his early twenties at the time. But whenever we turned around, there he was, eavesdropping and pretending to mop. I ran a background check on him, talked to his boss, checked him out. Nothing unusual. But he tripped all my alarms. When we interviewed him, he swore he hadn't seen anything. But he asked questions all the time about the investigation. Maybe I'm just a bitter old codger—I totally am—but I swear he always sounded like he hoped the killer was giving us a run for his money," Gordon replied.

"That sounds like our fanboy," Vic said. "Except I think he's acquired some new skills since then."

"What do you mean?" Gordon eyed Vic curiously.

Vic hesitated, unsure how much to say, then plunged in. "Remember—I'm the guy who's engaged to my psychic partner, so that counts as full disclosure. We think that our fanboy picked up some witchy talents that have enabled him to send cursed items to people important to the Slitter trial to take them off the game board."

"I've seen the news—you think that's what's behind what happened to the D.A. and the judge?"

Vic and Ross nodded. "Simon checked the items that triggered the events. Definitely malicious magic. But the Slitter didn't send them. So…"

"The janitor's name was Bert Judd. Wasn't from around here, but to my knowledge, he's still alive and still in South Carolina," Gordon said. "I kept tabs on him for a long time, but everything was quiet. If you're looking for a fanboy, I'd start with him."

"I have a friend who's an FBI profiler," Ross volunteered. "I asked him for information to better understand what kind of person becomes a serial killer groupie. Once he gets back to me, Judd is going to the top of the list."

"Judd isn't a janitor anymore. He runs a janitorial service company," Gordon said. "But from what I've been able to track, he favors occult and conspiracy channels on some of the dodgier social media. So the idea of him trying to put a hex on someone who was causing problems for his idol seems entirely in character to me."

Gordon rubbed the bridge of his nose as if to stave off a headache. "I'm going to have nightmares again, I'm sure of it."

Vic's ears pricked. "Are the bad dreams a constant, or did they get worse lately?" He figured it was a toss-up on whether their line of work caused permanent PTSD or that the dreams had another, darker cause.

Gordon frowned. "You know how the job goes. Can't unsee that stuff."

"We think there might be dark magic involved that feeds off fear," Vic said, not ready to bring up the idea of a "creature." "Sleep problems have become an epidemic since the Slitter trial started ramping up."

"Are you serious? Shit." Gordon looked sharply at Vic. "It's definitely much worse recently. Before, it would be maybe a couple of bad dreams a month. Sometimes, I'd go longer. But lately, it's almost every night. I'm not just remembering the worst of old cases—although that would be bad enough. Now my brain is running through every 'what if' that could have gone really wrong. Frankly—I'm exhausted."

"I understand completely," Ross agreed. "It's the same for me."

"If there's some outside power behind these dreams, do you know how to stop it?" Gordon asked.

"That's Simon's specialty," Vic replied. "He's pulled in the folks who know that sort of thing. I don't doubt that he'll figure it out."

"Well, don't take too long. I'm an old man, and I need my rest."

Ross cleared his throat, and Vic knew it was time to go. "Thank you for talking with us. One more thing. Simon has managed to communicate with a couple of the ghosts of the young women who died. They both indicated that their bodies were hidden in the 'caves.' Do you have any idea what they're talking about?"

"Caves?" Gordon repeated. "Around here? Not to my knowledge."

"Didn't one of them also say something about a castle?" Ross prompted.

Gordon looked up sharply. "Caves and a castle. Well now, that's different."

"You lost me," Vic admitted.

"You didn't grow up here, or if you did, you're too young to remember," Gordon replied. "Back in the seventies, there was an attraction that was a big deal down near the Boardwalk—Vampire Castle. It looked like a castle from the outside, and it was a combination haunted house, wax museum, light show, and gift shop. It closed for good in the late seventies."

"Where was it?" Vic pressed, feeling sure they were onto something.

"Near where Ripley's is now. It sat empty for a while—probably legal issues—and then they finally took down the facade. I think there's a gift shop on the first floor, and I don't know what they did with the attraction contents. It's still the original building; it just doesn't look like a castle anymore."

"And the caves?" Ross pressed.

"Inside the castle, there was a maze through spooky caves. You saw all kinds of classic monsters from the movies—Dracula, Frankenstein's monster, the Wolfman, the Mummy. Some guy played a real pipe organ on the weekends. There was fake fog and jump scares and strobe lights. Definitely the place to take a hot date if you wanted her glued to your side," Gordon recalled with a chuckle.

"Did the castle ever come up in your investigation? Was the building searched?" Vic didn't try to temper the excitement in his voice.

Gordon shook his head. "Not to my knowledge. No probable cause. It had already been closed for a few years when the disappearances happened, and we didn't have a link. It never came up."

"Did Bert Judd ever work there? It sounds like he might have floated around town as a janitor," Vic asked.

"If he did, nothing struck me as odd about it at the time," Gordon replied. "But then again, since the castle had been closed for years, it wouldn't have seemed relevant."

Vic and Ross exchanged a glance. "I'll get a warrant," Ross said, and Vic knew his partner recognized the glint in Vic's eye when he was on the hunt.

"Let me know what you find out," Gordon said. "About the castle and Judd. I'll go back through my private notes, and if anything jumps out at me—now that I know what you're looking for —I'll holler."

"Thank you," Vic said. "Sorry to intrude on your retirement."

Gordon shrugged. "Retirement is overrated. I miss the thrill of the chase, to tell you the truth. And I'd like to see those disappearances solved before I kick the bucket. I didn't like leaving the department with unsolved cases. Those poor women deserved better."

Vic and Ross promised to stay in touch and thanked Gordon again before heading to the car.

"Well, you found both the caves and the castle," Ross said as they headed back to the office. "I'd say that's a win."

"We need to find Judd," Vic replied. "He sounds like a top suspect for our fanboy."

"Go slow and do it right," Ross cautioned. "We don't want to get the evidence tossed on a technicality."

Vic rolled his eyes, but he realized that Ross was right. "I know. I know."

Ross took a turn and Vic frowned. "Where are you going?"

"I thought we'd drive by the Vampire Castle," Ross replied. "Been a while since I've paid attention to that part of the strip."

The old attraction wasn't far from where Grand Strand Ghost Tours was located on the Boardwalk, on a parallel street in a busy but older section of Myrtle Beach, a thicket of T-shirt and gift shops, ice cream parlors, arcades, and bars that catered to the karaoke college crowd.

When Vic first moved to the beach, he had spent his weekends seeing the sights, in part to stay busy and forget how far he was from his family in Pittsburgh. He'd dragged his new partner—Ross—with him when he could and went alone when that wasn't possible. That had provided a rough introduction to his adopted city and helped him pick up the vibe of a town so different from what he was used to.

Vic and Simon preferred checking out the historic sites, wandering the paths at the nearby sculpture garden, or walking the trails at Brookgreen Gardens. Just for the hell of it, they had managed to take in the very popular live musical shows at least once to see what all the fuss was about. Those were professionally produced but just as corny as Simon and Vic expected, targeted to the retiree snowbirds who wintered in the lower Carolinas.

Mini-golf at the many elaborate courses had also become something of a guilty pleasure for a night out.

"Kinda hard to imagine it looking like a castle, don't you think?" Vic observed as they slowed to pass the building that had once been home to the horror attraction.

"They can put a facade on anything—like the building they made look like it's upside-down," Ross said. "But it does sound like the old place had more style than some of the new haunted houses. It's the kind of thing I would have gone to when I was a teenager."

The building, which was next to a big oddities museum, looked plain enough. The T-shirt and gift shop—which had once been the street level entrance for Vampire's Castle—didn't differ much from its competitors, with a brightly colored awning and neon-hued painted windows offering special sales. An inflatable waving tube dancer drew the eye with bright colors and motion.

Vic's gaze traveled up to the second floor. Dark, grimy windows suggested that level might have remained abandoned despite the lower floor getting repurposed.

"When we get back to the office, I want to know everything there is to know about Vampire's Castle—who owned it, why it shut down, and why the building stayed in limbo for so long," Vic said. "Also need to find out who owns it now because I'm going to ask for a search warrant for evidence of murder victims or remains—and I want Simon with us when we go take a look." He paused. "I also want to know if Thompson or Judd ever worked there or had any connection."

Ross cocked his head as he spared a glance at the building, slowing down in traffic. "If the building was abandoned for a number of years and Thompson was familiar with it, he might have thought it was the perfect dumping ground. No one around to notice comings and goings or investigate odd noises—or smells."

Vic nodded. "That's what I was thinking. And if nobody uses the second floor, there'd be no reason for anyone to go poking around."

Ross's phone trilled, and he spoke a command to pick up the call. "Ross—it's Ted. Got a minute?"

"Sure," Ross replied, mouthing "my FBI contact" to Vic. "Vic's with me, and I'm going to ask him to take notes while I drive. What did you find out?"

"You sure like to throw a guy a challenge," Ted replied. "I talked to our profilers. The whole serial killer fan thing is surprisingly common. It's the allure of the bad boy dialed up to eleven. Blame it on 'forbidden fruit' or the rush of getting away with breaking the law—until you don't. Goes with the American fascination with outlaws."

"I can kinda see that," Ross allowed. "Although serial killers?"

"Tell me," Ted agreed. "And get this—most of the fans are women. Even though the killers did horrible things to their female victims. The fans think the killer was misunderstood, or had a rough life, or would change if loved enough. And in the fan's mind, they're the one who can tame the beast."

"Good luck with that," Vic muttered.

"I didn't say it was rational or sane, but it is what it is," Ted replied.

"How about fan*boys*?" Ross asked. "Guys who love the outlaw vibe and live vicariously through their idol."

"Not as common, but still real. Usually, it's a guy who has been picked on all his life for being nerdy, unattractive, or offbeat. Not that plenty of people like that don't live perfectly normal, well-adjusted lives," Ted hurried to add.

"So the fanboy is a misfit, maybe even living down to the stereotype of having a room in his mom's basement," Ted went on. "He looks up to guys with a lot of swagger and can't see through their bravado. Guys like him want to be badass rock stars. They hate men who seem to get women easily. Usually has a chip on his shoulder the size of Manhattan and a history of blaming other people for his problems."

"So paranoid loser mama's boy with a bad attitude who hero-worships bullies," Ross recapped. "Lovely," he added sarcastically.

"The outlaw part is the appeal," Ted emphasized. "The fanboy wants to break rules but is afraid of consequences, so he idolizes the killer for breaking *all* the rules and getting away with it. Even when the killer gets caught, they're still a rockstar to the fan because of all the media hype."

All of that made sense in a sick way to Vic. "Do the super fans ever try to insert themselves into the situation?" he asked. "Maybe they fancy themselves to be an accomplice, or they do things to harm the prosecution to help their hero?"

Ted paused. "Sounds like you've got a situation."

"Oh boy, do we ever," Ross muttered.

"That sort of thing is less common but not unheard of," Ted replied. "Most fans stick to letters or gifts. Sometimes they'll write to the judge to let the killer off, or they'll send letters to the editor."

"If the fan knew the killer even tangentially before the trial, they might write themselves into the story by thinking that they 'helped' by not tipping off the police—or the victims. That's a level of crazy that raises a lot of red flags," Ted warned. "And if you've got a fan who is making threats or taking actions to harm people they see as a threat to the killer, that's not just delusional—it's dangerous."

"Got it," Ross said. "Thanks, Ted. That helps a lot."

"Hey, Ted—any chance you could run a suspect through your database in case you turn up something our system doesn't?" Vic asked. "Name is Bert Judd. Not sure where he was born, but he's spent a lot of time in Myrtle Beach. Janitor. He's probably around sixty, and I'm guessing he checks off all the fanboy boxes. Anything you can tell us would help a lot."

"I'll see what I can do," Ted replied. "Talk to you soon."

"And while Ted's doing his FBI thing, I want to read over the results from the search I ran," Vic said, sitting back as Ross headed for the station.

"I'll bet you a box of donuts that Bert's clean," Ross replied. "All hat and no cattle as they say in Texas. Living in a fantasy world."

Vic frowned. "Yeah, but if he's sending the cursed objects, something's changed. Maybe he watched from afar with the eighties killer and even with the Slitter until Fischer got caught. Thompson got away with murder, but now Fischer's going to trial. Maybe Judd thinks his hero needs his help."

"And in the meantime, he's been brushing up on dark magic?"

"Plenty of people in these parts know about paying someone to 'put a root' on an enemy," Vic said. "Simon's friend Miss Eppie won't do curses, but you can bet there are other folks who'll do whatever a paying customer wants—which probably makes them even more dangerous because they might not be as skilled. Sloppy magic is like a homemade bomb. No telling how it's really going to work."

"Hey, Vic—this doesn't look good."

Vic's head snapped up as they approached the police station. More reporters than usual clustered around the front entrance as an ambulance carefully edged its way through the press of bodies. Flash photos and video cameras crowded the rescue vehicle, and the journalists didn't yield easily as uniformed officers attempted to clear a path.

"Fuck," Vic muttered. "What now?"

The uniforms held back the tide of bodies to let Ross pull into the lot. Even with the windows rolled up, Vic could hear them shouting.

"Can you give us a statement?"

"Is the Slitter trial cursed?"

"Is it true someone is working hoodoo against the Prosecution?"

"How did the Myrtle Beach Police Department lose control of the situation?"

Thankfully, the heavily tinted windows kept the crowd from seeing inside, but Vic could make out the microphones and cameras as well as the faces of the reporters. He recognized several from the evening news but didn't see Walt among them.

Vic and Ross ignored the shouts outside the gate as they hurried through the station's back door. Vic's heart sank when they entered. It didn't take a psychic to read the room, not with the expressions of fear and confusion on every face.

"What happened? Who got hurt?" Ross barked.

"Captain Hargrove had a serious allergic reaction," Stu Decker told them, a patrol officer who often worked cases with them.

"To what?" Vic questioned. "He never said anything about allergies."

Ross shook his head. "I don't remember knowing he had any."

Decker shrugged. "Well, that's sure what it looked like. He went down fast, started swelling up, couldn't breathe. One of the guys called 911, and the dispatcher said to use an EpiPen. The ambulance got here in minutes—you just missed all the excitement."

"What was Cap doing right before he got hit?" Vic asked.

Decker gestured toward Hargrove's office. "Paperwork, going through his mail. There hasn't been time to pick up when he dropped everything."

"Don't touch anything," Ross ordered. "There's a good chance whatever triggered the reaction is with those envelopes."

"You mean like back when someone mailed anthrax?" Decker asked.

"Sort of," Vic hedged. He glanced at Ross. "I hate to drag Simon through the gauntlet out there, but we need him to look at the stuff." *Why didn't Hargrove's hex bag protect him? Or didn't he have it on him since he felt safe inside the station?*

"Call him, and I'll arrange a patrol car to pick him up," Ross replied. "That'll make it easier to get him past the cameras."

"Stu—can you keep us updated on how the captain is doing? He doesn't need the whole squad down there, but if there's anything we can do to help, we need to know," Vic said.

"I'm on it," Decker promised.

Within half an hour, Simon arrived. "Is Hargrove okay?" he asked as soon as he spotted Vic and Ross.

"Stu's staying in touch with the hospital," Vic answered. "All we know is that he's not in danger, and they don't want visitors yet."

"What do you need me to look at?" Simon followed Vic and

Ross to Hargrove's office. Envelopes littered the floor, sealed except for one small padded mailer which had been torn open.

"I'm going to take a wild guess and say that might be the one with the cursed object." Simon bent over the mailer, careful not to touch. He frowned, looking at the item that lay half out of the envelope. "Looks like a bass lure. Does Hargrove fish?"

"Yeah, whenever he gets the chance," Ross replied. "I think he's even entered a few fly fishing competitions."

Vic swore under his breath. "It's bad enough that someone's mailing cursed items, but picking things that tie into a favorite hobby is a level of creepy stalker."

Ross nodded. "It's intentionally invasive, like saying 'I know all kinds of things about you.'"

"It's the same resonance as with the card, ticket, and—I'd bet—the poker chip. Want to bet there's a fishing pro who lost a competition because he went into anaphylactic shock?"

Simon ran his hand above the other mail and pronounced it harmless. He squatted by the lure, staring intently at the neatly typed address label. "Whoever's behind this has enough skill to make a highly personalized curse. An amateur would have used a general hex that affected every postal worker who touched the envelope. But we haven't heard of that happening with any of the incidents."

"Does that mean it's safe for anyone but Hargrove to touch it?" Ross asked, sidling up behind Simon for a better look.

"I'd rather err on the side of caution. Too many people have a little psychic ability that they don't realize or acknowledge, and we have no idea how the curse would affect them," Simon replied. "I wouldn't want someone like Cassidy to touch it, that's for sure."

Simon's cousin, Cassidy Kincaide, was a psychometric who could read the history and magic of an object by touching it. Vic shuddered, thinking what effect the curse would have on a person with that kind of ability.

"I've been using wooden tongs to get our mail out of the box and then dumping it into a warded circle on the deck before I go through it," Simon added. "Nothing's turned up yet, but given how prominent a role Vic and I played—thanks to the media—I can't imagine the fanboy won't want to warn us both off."

Ross turned to Vic. "We need to get the word out to the jurors and other essential team members for the prosecution to have someone else handle all the mail and not to let them touch any unexpected objects."

"And how, exactly, do you plan to explain that?" Vic challenged.

Ross shrugged. "Just like Stu said—blame it on anthrax, or ricin, or cooties. As long as no one else goes to the hospital. Then we collect the items and keep building that database of people from their hobby groups."

"Want to bet we find Bert Judd in all the groups under different aliases?" Vic countered.

"That wouldn't surprise me at all," Ross replied.

While they waited for someone from the evidence locker to collect the lure and envelope, Vic and Ross filled Simon in on what they had learned from Gordon.

"While we wait for your warrant, I'll see what I can pick up from the ghosts. Maybe Dante can scout the Vampire Castle building for us. That could be helpful," Simon mused.

"Talk to the dead people all you want, but please, Simon, stay away from the building until we all go together. Judd's out there, and even if you don't know who he is, I guarantee he knows who you are," Vic said. "Don't take chances—he's nuts and definitely dangerous."

"Agreed," Simon replied. "I won't go looking for trouble."

Vic believed his fiancé. He just hoped trouble didn't go looking for them.

6

SIMON

Vic and Ross headed to work early, intending to check on Captain Hargrove. Simon made them promise to let him know how Hargrove was doing. Simon finished his coffee before heading over to The Golden Strand to talk with Leanne, Michelle's friend who remembered Lisa Murdock, one of the girls who vanished.

On the way to the hotel, Simon pondered what Vic and Ross had learned from John Gordon. Ross had warned that they might not get the warrant to explore the old Vampire Castle until tomorrow since a forty-year-old case didn't qualify as urgent. Still, the reasoning that pointed to Thompson as the long-ago killer and the fake caves of the old haunted attraction as their final resting place seemed solid.

Simon wasn't sure what he hoped to find out from Leanne or Ed Gallagher, the retired reporter he and Walt planned to visit that afternoon. But he had learned to trust his instinct, and his gut reminded him that suspicions alone didn't mean a case was solved. If the interviews didn't shed new light on the murders, at least Simon could tell himself that he'd been thorough.

"Hiya, Simon." Michelle wasn't on duty, but she had promised to meet Simon to make introductions.

"Sorry to make you come in on your day off," he said. Simon had a tray with three large lattes from Le Miz since Michelle had clued him in that a good java was the key to Leanne's heart.

"Not like I'm working a shift," Michelle replied with a shrug. "I'm going to run errands after this and then go home and binge-watch my favorite shows." Simon passed her the cup with the sugar-free vanilla syrup she preferred.

"Leanne is expecting us. I told her a little about you so she wouldn't be blindsided." Michelle took a few sips and gave a satisfied moan.

"Good?" Simon asked, laughing.

Michelle sighed contentedly. "Oh yeah. Fine coffee is a thing of beauty."

"So Leanne didn't freak out over talking to a ghost whisperer?" Simon's tone held a note of self-mocking.

"Please. We're in the Lowcountry. People here *believe*."

Michelle and Simon ducked through a "staff only" door into the service corridors that ran behind the areas guests saw. They passed the back entrance to the kitchen, then headed deeper into the interior of the hotel until they reached the large laundry facility.

They stopped at an office door with the plaque that read *Leanne North, Director of Housekeeping*. Michelle knocked. Simon cocked his head, trying to tune into the low buzz of energies his abilities picked up.

"Come in."

Leanne sat behind an old desk that looked like a post-war relic. Close-cropped white hair accentuated her dark skin. Her lined face and corded neck suggested her age, but the ram-rod straight posture, strong forearms, and imperious lift to her head made it clear Leanne dealt with age—and life—on her own terms.

"This is for you," Simon said, holding out the third coffee, which Leanne accepted with a pleased smile.

"Miss North—" Michelle began.

"Y'all call me Leanne." She had the heavy drawl of a

Lowcountry native, with a measured cadence that made each word important. Leanne looked Simon up and down. "Miss Eppie speaks highly of you, Simon."

As soon as he entered the office, Simon placed the frisson of power from hoodoo protections. He suspected that gris-gris bags, a sprinkling of red brick dust, and other root work contributed to the strong sense of calm safety inside the small office.

"You know each other?"

She laughed, a low rumble. "Oh, yes. For a very long time. She is blessed with special gifts, and I consider her to be a wise counselor." Leanne gestured toward the two wooden chairs across from her desk. "Please, sit. Ask your questions. I'll tell you what I recall."

Simon and Michelle took their seats, and Simon looked up. "Do you remember Lisa Murdock?"

Leanne's dark eyes grew sad. "I do. That poor, lost girl. Evil took her."

"I know it was a long time ago, but we might have new information that could help us bring closure to Lisa's death and the other women who disappeared back then."

"You've seen her ghost? You know she's dead?"

Simon shook his head. "I haven't talked with Lisa's spirit, but I did talk to others from the group that went missing. I don't have any doubt that Lisa died not long after she vanished."

Leanne sighed but didn't look surprised. "I wanted to hope for better, but deep down I always knew."

Since Leanne embraced the root work protections, Simon wondered if she had a touch of heightened intuition as well. He questioned whether Thompson used magic to trap his victims or merely the sick skills of a predator.

"What do you remember about Lisa's disappearance? Did anything unusual happen around that time?"

Leanne stared into the distance for a while before answering. "Lisa came here from a very small town. I worried about her because she wasn't street smart, not the way some of the girls were. Myrtle Beach isn't Las Vegas or Atlantic City, but there's bad here with the good, just the same."

She hesitated. "The last time I saw her was when she got on the evening shuttle. I felt a chill like someone walked across my grave. I tried to call out to her, but the door closed, and the bus took off. Then, she was gone."

"You said she was *lost?*" Simon prompted.

Leanne nodded. "I suspected she was a runaway. She was like a stray dog that wants attention but doesn't get too close because they've been kicked. I tried to encourage her where I could, but this is a big hotel and a large staff, and we didn't cross paths often."

"So no one looked for her?"

"I called her when she didn't show up for her shift. When she didn't answer, I stopped by her apartment, but the landlady said she didn't know anything."

Simon recalled Vic saying that the retired detective suspected the landlady as an accomplice—or at least someone willing to look the other way.

"Did you ever pick up any hint of anything spooky around Lisa?"

A secret smile spread across Leanne's face. "Are you asking if I thought someone put a root on her?"

"More or less."

"No. If I had thought that, I would have gotten Eppie involved." Leanne shook her head. "This was a different kind of darkness— true evil. I caught the sense of it now and again late at night, around the time the shift ended. I didn't know where it came from or how to fight it." She looked down. "I was afraid. Perhaps if I had…"

Simon shook his head. "There was nothing you could have done. He might have taken you as well."

"No. I wasn't what he wanted. Those girls were so young…"

"I'm sorry to bring back bad memories." Simon paused. "Did you ever pay attention to the shuttle driver? Or a young janitor who was a little too interested?"

Leanne frowned. "There were several drivers. I never paid attention to them. As for the janitors—they came and went. But I do remember one who made me uncomfortable. He wasn't here long. I asked for him to be removed. He had bad energy. I didn't want him in the building."

"Do you remember his name?"

Leanne shook her head. "It was a long time ago, and he didn't stay. I don't know. I'm sorry."

Simon didn't doubt Judd was the creepy janitor or that it was Thompson's dark obsession that set off Leanne's senses. What she said was confirmation enough.

"Find them." Leanne leaned forward and met his gaze with intense, dark eyes. "Let them come home."

"We will," Simon promised. He hoped he could keep his word.

———

Simon met Walt and his friend in Le Mizzenmast. Tracey had purchased a bankrupt pirate museum to turn it into a bakery and coffee shop but couldn't afford to remodel. Instead, she kept the privateer theme and made it her brand.

"So this is a Dread Pirate Roberts?" Walt sipped the latte that was Tracey's signature specialty.

"Yep. It's my favorite," Simon replied, savoring his cup.

"I can see why." Ed Gallagher agreed. "I remember this place when it was a tourist attraction. It's way better as a coffeehouse."

The slightly built man with a gray goatee and thinning hair looked more like a musician than a former reporter. Then again, Simon thought, Ed's uber-nebbishness made him unthreatening and easy to talk to.

"Pirates didn't look like that. Bad teeth, scurvy, and they smelled really awful." Simon's ghostly ancestor Dante had come along for the ride, curious about the museum. He had also been willing to slip inside the second floor of the old Vampire Castle after their meeting.

"You're going to ruin all my illusions," Simon returned silently.

"Now that you've plied me with good coffee, what do you want to know?" Ed asked.

"Anything you remember about the young women who disappeared in the early eighties?" Simon asked.

Ed took a bite of a fresh-baked chocolate croissant and closed his eyes in bliss. "This is really good." After he finished the pastry, Ed returned his attention to Simon and Walt.

"I remember that the victims were all far too young to die." He sobered quickly. "I fed tips to Detective John Gordon, except for the ones he wouldn't believe."

"Try me," Simon replied. "I've seen a lot of strange things."

"I looked you up before I agreed to come. If you're the real deal, then I bet you have."

"He's real," Walt vouched for Simon.

"Don't say I didn't warn you," Ed said with a shrug. "I retraced the last known steps of the missing women after the cops were done. We were never sure exactly where the victims were grabbed, but we knew where someone had seen them last. I realized that in each case, about six feet away, there was a strange symbol chalked nearby."

He took another sip of coffee. "The symbols weren't flashy. They weren't meant to be noticed—someone made an effort for them to blend in. But once I noticed them, I started looking for more. When I took a sketch to a witchy friend of mine, she said it was a binding spell. Like a magical roofie. They didn't seem to affect anyone after the kidnapping, so maybe they were one-time-use, or perhaps the person who marked them had to be present."

"Do you remember what the symbols looked like?" Simon found himself holding his breath.

"Figured you'd ask." Ed took a piece of paper from his jacket pocket and spread it out on the table between them. "Here you go, best that I remember."

Simon didn't recognize the sigil, but he intended to keep an eye out for it from now on. "Thank you." He frowned. "You found symbols, but the cops didn't care? Or you didn't think the cops would listen?"

"Gordon and I had a good rapport. I didn't want to ruin it if he thought I was a nutcase," Ed replied. "Don't forget—the whole 'Satanic Panic' was just ramping up. People started seeing devil worshippers and crazy cultists under every rock. Serious journalists steered clear, as did cops who thought the whole thing was a witch hunt. So I investigated on my own and stayed quiet, hoping I'd find something irrefutable."

"But you didn't." Simon guessed.

"It was beyond refute in my mind." Ed lifted his chin defiantly. "But this being South Carolina, my friends who had unusual 'talents' were deep underground for their own safety. They could have lost their jobs, their homes, and been hauled in on trumped-up charges. There was no internet, so research meant books. I could have gotten fired if my editor had ever found out what I was doing."

Simon sat back, his coffee forgotten for the moment. "What did you figure out, aside from the binding spell?"

"I think the killer was self-taught. Probably someone who took horror movies a little too seriously and then was unlucky enough to happen into real sources. I also don't think he took the women for sex, which went against all the police theories," Ed answered. "You ever hear of Lady Bathory?"

"The crazy aristocrat who bathed in blood to stay young?" Walt put in.

Ed nodded. "I figured the person taking the women was working some sort of rejuvenation spell. Not to stay young—to extend his life, or cure a condition that medicine at the time couldn't."

"Like cancer." They both looked at Simon, who cleared his throat. "Gordon's top suspect died of cancer."

"Exactly," Ed agreed. "I think he used the murders to stave off the inevitable until he couldn't function anymore."

"Did he have a Renfield?" Simon asked, hoping Ed got the Dracula reference.

"You mean a crazy, willing servant? There was this kid who always seemed to be around when the police investigated another disappearance. At first, I thought he was just into crime voyeurism —there are plenty like that. But after a while, I thought it was odd. He was a little too interested—and he seemed to be rooting against the police," Ed told them.

"Did you get a name?"

Ed nodded. "Bert Judd. I just couldn't come up with something to report him for that would stick. Gordon didn't like the kid either, but being creepy isn't a crime."

"Are you following the Slitter case?" Simon questioned.

"Who isn't?" Ed replied, and Walt nodded.

"Then you've seen the headlines about bad luck befalling some key players. I don't believe in luck. I think someone is sabotaging the trial because they've got some hero-worship going for Fischer," Simon told them. "And Judd is at the top of my list."

"I agree with you—although now as then, I can't prove it," Ed said. "I knew as soon as the nightmares came back that this whole mess was starting again."

"Tell me about the nightmares." Simon leaned in.

"Like cops and EMTs, reporters see a lot of awful stuff as part of the job." Ed drained the dregs from his cup. "So bad dreams go with the press pass. But in the thick of the disappearances, the dreams took on a whole new level of intensity. It felt like something was sitting on my chest, sucking out my life. I couldn't move. I could barely breathe. It was like an assault—only there was no one there."

"Did other people have dreams as well?"

Ed nodded. "Yeah, I heard the victims' families, and even the cops mention it. My grandmother said it must be a boo hag and to paint my porch ceiling 'haint blue' to make it go away."

Boo hag, Simon mentally filed away. *I need to look into that.*

"Be careful, Simon," Ed warned. "You seem like a decent guy—heart in the right place and all that. But you aren't just up against serial killers and crazy fanboys and maybe a nightmare monster. Myrtle Beach is owned by developers and promoters. Murders—and murder trials—are bad for tourism. There are rich, powerful people who will exert pressure to be done with the bad press and then sweep it under the rug as fast as possible."

"Gordon had to put up with a lot of that," Walt agreed. "And if your detective partner hasn't run into that already, don't be surprised when it happens. Those power brokers don't need a connection to the killer to be inadvertently working in his favor."

Simon thought Vic had mentioned something about the town fathers prodding to get the trial relocated for publicity's sake. While they didn't condone murder, they were definitely more concerned with profits than justice.

"Thank you both. You've given me a lot to work with," Simon told them.

"Call me if you think of more questions," Ed told him, sliding his card across the table.

Simon gave him one for the store. "And if you remember anything else, give me a buzz."

Walt and Ed were clearly going to talk shop, so Simon said goodbye and headed down the block toward where Vampire's Castle used to be.

"Have I told you that there was nothing at all romantic about being a pirate?" Dante said, remaining out of sight but present in Simon's mind.

"Many times." Simon tried to hide his grin, enjoying teasing his ancestor.

"Brackish water, wormy biscuits, storms at sea, and if the King's Navy wasn't chasing them, then privateers like Coltt and I were breathing down their necks. Pirates were not nice people—and not nearly as good looking or well-dressed as in that horrible movie you made me watch."

"I didn't force you to do anything. And it's still one of the most profitable movies of all time," Simon needled.

"This generation has no taste." Dante sighed, but Simon knew the spirit had been riveted to the screen the night they'd watched the first movie in the series. Unfortunately, Dante couldn't share the popcorn.

"That's it," Simon murmured under his breath as he stopped across the street from the defunct attraction. Despite his promise to Vic to stay out of trouble, he felt as safe here as anywhere on the Grand Strand. A popular oddities museum sat next door to what was now a T-shirt shop with an unused second floor, and even though it wasn't tourist season, plenty of visitors still walked this stretch in daylight looking for diversions.

"So we went from pretend pirates to pretend vampires? You live in a very strange time," Dante commented.

"You have no idea," Simon replied. *"Can you get inside and go to the*

second floor? If we're right, there will be bodies from forty years ago, and maybe some stuff the killer kept that belonged to the victims."

"Unless it's warded against ghosts, I should be able to have a look around," Dante replied. *"I'll keep an eye out for spirits. Is it said to be haunted? Because from what you say, it should be."*

Simon shook his head. *"I keep pretty close tabs on the known hauntings, and this location hasn't come up—either in the past or since the castle closed. Which makes me wonder…"*

"Let's see what I can find. Then afterward, you can take me to some more places that aren't real." With that snarky comment, Dante left. Simon pretended to window shop in the nearest tourist trap, trying to kill time without obviously loitering.

If Judd had been a janitor at Vampire's Castle before it closed, maybe he held onto a key. We still don't know Thompson's connection to the place. Did he work there before he took up killing? That would make sense, but it's probably hard to find a paper trail after all this time.

When Dante didn't return immediately, Simon felt exposed hanging around on the street. He ducked into an ice cream shop and had just emerged with a butter pecan cone when he felt Dante's presence.

"Found them."

"What—?"

"The second floor looks like someone just blew out the candles and shut the door," Dante reported. *"There are false caves made out of something that looks like stone and isn't. They don't look much like real caverns, either."*

"What else?" Simon prompted.

"Someone made a hole in the false stone and hid the bodies inside, then put a larger 'rock' in front to hide it. Six corpses. More like mummies now."

"Shit." Simon felt relieved that they had found the missing women's bodies but sad to confirm their deaths.

"Several ghosts remain. Perhaps the ones you contacted were able to leave the building and are stronger—the ones left behind are barely a flicker."

"Did you see anything that might have been the killer's trophies? Jewelry, personal items, shoes, pieces of clothing?"

"They're arranged on a small table like a shrine. But…it appears someone

has been there recently. The dust had been disturbed, and there were footprints. The shrine looked tended."

"Well, that's not good." Simon licked a drip from his momentarily forgotten cone. *"Did you learn anything from the ghosts?"*

Simon picked up on Dante's emotions and felt his distress.

"They're frightened of the building's visitor and afraid there will be more murders. Some of the ghosts have started to lose their sense of self. It supports your theory that the killer leeched energy from their deaths to heal himself. And I picked up a phrase—'no surrender.'"

"Do you know what they mean?"

"They are united in defying their killer's desire to make them disappear. I had the sense that he bound them somehow to that place so they couldn't move on to the afterlife."

"Guess it turned out to be a 'vampire's castle' after all, but not in the way anyone expected," Simon noted.

"I told the ghosts you and Vic were coming and that you were the good guys," Dante offered. *"And Simon—be careful. While I didn't encounter him, the ghosts warned me that Thompson's spirit also haunts the building. He's just as much a madman dead as he was alive."*

"Thank you." As glad as Simon felt to have a break in the cold case, his heart ached for the families of the victims and for the young women who came to the beach and found death.

Dante's spirit blinked out. Simon had grown used to the ghost's coming and going, and Vic had come to accept that sometimes the spirit of a Revolutionary War-era privateer showed up for movie night.

Simon's thoughts spun as he walked back to the store, savoring his ice cream. Everything he'd learned in a very busy morning crowded his brain. He couldn't wait to talk it out with Vic and put the pieces together from what they'd learned through various sources.

Thompson didn't keep trophies at his house. Maybe the cops will find evidence in the old Vampire's Castle tying him to the murders. That would help with closure—for the families and the cops.

Even better if we could find something that shows Judd knows about the old killings. Unfortunately, he's probably too slick to leave that kind of evidence behind. But he'll slip up sometime. They all do.

Simon picked up a pizza to take back to the shop since he and Pete would both need lunch. He couldn't tell Pete much about an active police investigation, but he did assure him that the morning's interviews had been useful.

"I thought I saw that Judd guy go by on the boardwalk," Pete volunteered.

Simon glanced up, worried. "What did he do?"

"Just walked. I wouldn't have thought much of it, except that you'd shown me his picture, and I'm sure he's who I saw," Pete replied before he took another bite of the melted cheese threatening to slip from his slice.

Simon had warned Pete about Judd. It seemed inevitable that Simon would draw the malicious fanboy's attention. He'd given Pete dire warnings about handling the mail and told him what to look for based on the other cursed objects.

They'd realized that the curses had to be highly personalized, or else the envelopes could never have made it through the postal system without leaving a wake of injured people. That meant keeping an eye out for odd pieces specifically addressed to Simon or Pete.

"Did he try to come inside? Peer through the window?" Simon asked. It seemed in character for Judd to linger outside, casing the shop.

Pete shook his head. "No. He didn't stay long, either. But for probably fifteen minutes, he just hung out near the fence and stared at the storefront across the boardwalk. He didn't do anything—which was even creepier. I couldn't figure out if he wanted me to see him to send a message or if he was sizing us up for something."

"Great," Simon said with a sigh. "You did the right thing not trying to engage him. Inside, you've got the wardings to protect you."

"Is this another time where I need to stay in the apartment upstairs until the danger blows over? Because I don't know how to explain that to Mikki."

Simon managed a chuckle. "I don't think we're to that point—yet. Just keep your eyes open and that hex bag I gave you in your pocket."

After Pete took his break, Simon went to the office. He sent emails to Travis Dominick and Teag Logan, two of the most knowledgeable people he knew when it came to lore.

Travis was an ex-priest and former member of a secret Vatican demon-hunting group called the Sinistram. He knew a lot about magic—forbidden and otherwise—as well as having a scarily encyclopedic knowledge of supernatural creatures. Teag was the best friend of Simon's cousin Cassidy in Charleston. His magic made him a hell of a hacker, and he'd had plenty of first-hand experience fighting monsters of all kinds.

If anyone would know of a creature that fed off fear and how to kill it, it would be Travis and Teag. And Teag was also Simon's best bet to find out about Judd. Both of them might know more about the strange sigils that Ed had found chalked near the long-ago disappearances.

Once Simon shot off the emails, he felt a weight lift from his shoulders. Dante had verified the existence of the bodies and the ghosts—as well as the personal items on the shrine. If something went awry with the search warrant or the building owner decided to cover up what happened, Simon didn't doubt that Dante and the ghosts would find a way to preserve the scene until it could be properly documented.

Once that was done, Simon checked the time, slumped in his chair, and let his head fall back. He and Vic were supposed to leave work early to check out the Train Depot for its decor, see if they could imagine themselves holding their reception there, and review the contract and calendar.

Maybe if I just rest my eyes…

A featureless shadow man stalked him down darkened corridors. No matter where he turned or how fast he ran, the figure remained just a few strides behind him.

Simon startled awake from dark dreams. Disoriented, he looked wildly around before finally realizing where he was. "Fuck, that's embarrassing."

"You okay, boss?" Pete called. "I've got a bucket of cold water handy if you need it."

"I'm good, thanks." Simon shivered at the thought. "How's everything out front?"

"Too quiet," Pete called out. "We need more people to come in and browse. Maybe we should mix things up a bit. People think they know what we've got for sale, and they only see a fraction from the window."

"I'm up for moving things around, changing the displays," Simon replied, venturing out of the office. "If you've got ideas, go ahead."

"Are you still going to that appointment you set up online?" Pete asked. "With Vic?"

"Assuming the world hasn't imploded, I'm supposed to meet him at the Train Depot, tour the site, grab dinner, and come back in time to do my ghost tour tonight," Simon replied.

"Then you'd better be going. It's later than you think," Pete replied, holding up his phone to reveal the time.

"Shit. You're right. See you in a bit." Simon grabbed his jacket and headed out. He remembered to pause to check for reporters or Judd and let out a sigh of relief when the boardwalk appeared to be clear of stalkers.

Simon picked Vic up from the block behind the police department, where he'd managed to evade the reporters.

"You doin' okay?" Simon asked as Vic slumped in his seat and closed his eyes.

"Peachy." Vic sounded dead tired. "Just a long fuckin' day."

"I can postpone—"

Vic shook his head without bothering to open his eyes. "No. There will always be something. And with the way most places book up, if we put off making a choice, we could be waiting ten years to get hitched."

Simon reached over and placed a hand on Vic's thigh. "We can do the vows anywhere, anytime. What we're looking for is the reception venue."

Vic snorted. "You think my mother is going to do without seeing us walk down some sort of aisle? Think again. Just because we can't have a High Mass does not mean Mama D'Amato is going to be done out of a proper wedding for her son."

Simon laughed. "Glad we have our priorities straight."

"Probably the only 'straight' thing about this wedding," Vic joked.

"I mean, I'm sure we could rent out Aloha Cowboy if we asked nicely," Simon teased back. The iconic gay bar had been a storied part of the Grand Strand's history, and showing up there at least once was a rite of passage, even if the club scene didn't appeal to either Simon or Vic.

Vic groaned. "Yeah, I can see explaining to my eighty-five-year-old great-aunt—*Sister* Maria Antonia—why the bar area is named 'The Wet Spot.'"

Simon chuckled. "On the other hand, it would pretty much guarantee my parents won't try to crash the party. Having a roving photographer posting party photos online of the guests would do more to keep my mother away than all the hex bags in the Lowcountry."

Vic had already experienced Gloria Kincaide at her worst when she had tried to manipulate Simon into returning to the university and his ex-fiancé. While his mother made a show of accepting her gay son, she had also always urged Simon to "look as straight as possible."

"Really? I might reconsider, despite my auntie nun," Vic teased.

"We could make sure the bartenders wear their 'formal' leather," Simon continued. "The party favors might be memorable."

Vic opened one eye and glared at him. "You're doing this so I'll agree to anything else, right?"

Simon managed a look of complete innocence as exaggerated as it was fake. "Just presenting options."

Vic flipped him off and closed his eyes again.

"Later, if you're good." Simon laughed.

He parked in front of the old brick building and paused to take a closer look. The rectangular depot still had the roof overhang that gave it a distinctly 'train station' profile. Although tracks remained in front, the trains had stopped running years ago.

Vic stepped up beside him. "What do you think?"

"I like that it's kinda different. Let's have a look at the inside."

"You must be Simon and Vic!" A young dark-haired woman with a ponytail and a clipboard hurried out to meet them. "I'm Kara, and I can't wait to show you around."

Kara led them toward the entrance. "The Depot was built in 1937, a year before Myrtle Beach officially became a town. The trains stopped running in 1967, and the depot became a warehouse. A community effort brought it back from ruin and raised the money to refurbish it into an event venue."

With a flourish, Kara rolled back the big bay door. "You're in luck—we're setting up for a retirement party, so you can get an idea of how the space can be dressed up."

"Wow," Simon murmured. He looked up at the original wooden trusses that had been draped with swags of twinkle lights. Exposed brick walls and a refinished plank floor maintained the historic feel. The interior was one large space, but from the tables set up, Simon could tell they'd have enough room for their guest list.

"We work with all the major caterers in town, as well as the bakeries and DJs," Kara assured them. "We have a clause in our contracts that forbids discrimination, so I can guarantee you won't have any 'cake' issues."

She swept through the space, greeting the workers who were busy setting up round tables. "We can get flowers, balloons, ice sculptures—whatever you want. We've also got sheer curtains that can soften the look of the brick if you prefer. We have a portable dance floor and a great sound system. Heck—we can hang a disco ball if you want one."

"Do people ever have the ceremony here as well as the reception?" Vic asked.

Kara nodded enthusiastically. "Oh yes. There's a lovely gazebo we use for the vows that can be rolled away afterward. It looks very good in photographs. And we can supply a non-denominational officiant as part of the package, or you can arrange that on your own."

Simon found himself holding his breath as Kara walked them around the depot, filling in details about the location's history and the way events were handled. He watched his fiancé's body language and started to relax as Vic asked more questions.

Vic hadn't gone into cop mode with sharp questions that made a discussion feel like an interrogation. Instead, he seemed to be enjoying the conversation and was as interested in the background as he was the mechanics of hosting an event.

"How far out are you booked?" Simon crossed his fingers in his pocket.

"Normally, it's a year to a year and a half," Kara told them. "But we aren't scheduled quite so far out right now, more like eleven months, and if you want sooner, sometimes we do get cancellations."

"We aren't prepared to sign today, but can you please walk us through the costs and the contract?" Simon asked. He and Vic had agreed in advance that no matter how much they liked any venue, they wouldn't be talked into committing on the spot. Simon hadn't changed his mind on taking a logical approach.

Yet the longer Kara talked, the more excited Simon felt. He couldn't read Vic's expression; rather, he didn't want to assume that what he read into the look on his boyfriend's face was accurate. But it seemed to Simon that Vic was enthusiastic about the depot as well.

Vic was the one trained to watch micro expressions during inter-rogation. But Simon had a lifetime of needing to pay close attention to body language to navigate the mercurial moods of a narcissistic mother as well as ruthless academic politics. He had studied Vic's face during a range of emotions, and he saw how Vic leaned forward into Kara's space to review the contract, how alight his eyes were as he asked detailed questions about decorations and catering.

Vic was in love, and not just with Simon. Something about the depot had captured his imagination. Simon was glad that he felt the same way because he wouldn't have wanted to disappoint his partner.

Simon had already gone through the contract and details online. He had run the numbers and knew the location was within their budget and would hold their expected guest list. But he had promised himself that he wouldn't get his heart set on any venue until he'd seen it in person and been able to discuss it with Vic. Now, he had the sense that their discussion might be relatively short.

"If you think of any other questions, please call me," Kara said as she walked them out. "I included a list of recent wedding clients you can call as a reference. If you trust the depot with your special day, I know we can make it memorable for all the right reasons."

They thanked her and headed back to the car. Both men were quiet until they were nearly back to the bungalow.

"Well?" Simon asked, suddenly worried he had misread Vic's reaction.

Vic grinned. "I think it's perfect, and my fiancé is a genius."

"Yeah?"

"It's got loads more personality than a regular hotel. I love the idea of a train depot because we're starting a journey together. There's history—which is catnip to you. Kara had good ideas for the decorations and gave us options—it wasn't one-size-fits-all. I got the feeling that whatever we came up with—within reason—they'd do their best to make happen."

"Is that a yes?"

Vic nodded, looking happy and slightly nauseous. "Yes."

Simon grinned, then pulled the car over to the curb so he could draw Vic into a celebratory kiss. Vic responded with quiet fervor, cupping the back of Simon's head with one hand.

Reluctantly, Simon finally drew back. "We'd better keep moving. We can seal the deal at home."

"I thought you had a tour tonight."

"I do. But there's always time for good communication," Simon replied with a wink.

"What about dinner?"

"I'll take something with me."

Given the choice between a slow dinner or slow love making, Simon didn't need to think twice. He could tell that Vic shared his mingled excitement and apprehension. Making plans meant that getting married was real—a forever commitment. While making that promise to Vic was what Simon wanted with all his heart, the gravity of the situation nearly made him pass out.

Tonight, every touch affirmed a vow, and each surge of pleasure confirmed the rightness of their union. Simon had heard people talk about sex as a form of communication, but it truly felt like he and Vic spoke volumes without words.

When they were both sated, Simon lay back amid the tousled covers with Vic's head pillowed against his chest.

"We should take a shower before we stick together. I can't go lead a ghost tour with sex hair—or smelling like sweat and jizz."

"You're adorable with sex hair, and I like the way you smell. So sue me—I'm a little possessive," Vic returned and licked Simon's chest for good measure.

"Don't start that, or we'll never get out of bed, and I'll die from starvation."

"I prefer to think that you had such a mind-blowing orgasm that you're still a bit woozy."

Simon's stomach rumbled loudly. "Apparently my orgasm is growling." He poked Vic lightly in the side. "C'mon. Let's shower and go for round two. I can eat a protein bar in the car on the way to the shop."

After they were done in the shower, Vic had enough time to make a sandwich and push it and a can of soda into Simon's hands.

"I'm coming with you," Vic announced, grabbing a couple of bars and a drink for himself before following Simon out the door.

"Love to have the company, but you've seen this tour several times. Why now?"

Vic shrugged. "Look, Judd's on the loose out there, and we aren't a hundred percent sure he's behind the cursed objects. If I stay home, I won't be able to concentrate because I'll be worrying about you. So if I'm not going to get anything done, I might as well not do it together. If you know what I mean."

Simon leaned in to kiss him. "I'm fine with that. Just don't come whining to me when you're bored."

"I don't whine."

"Excuse me. I should have said bitching and moaning."

"Bite me."

"I just did. You'll have to wait for round three," Simon replied with a smirk.

Simon and Pete both led popular ghost tours but with very different styles. Pete made his a performance, complete with costumes and dramatic storytelling. Simon's were more of a factual conversation without embellishment.

They offered several themes—pirates, historic ghosts, protective spirits. Both tourists and locals were repeat customers and happily purchased T-shirts, mugs, and other Grand Strand Ghost Tours souvenirs, along with Simon's books.

Thanks to Dante's coaching, Simon's pirate and privateer tour was a big favorite, often praised for getting obscure details right. Then again, other tour guides didn't have an ancestor ghost riding shotgun and whispering things only someone who lived at the time would know.

Tonight was a small group, only six people. That enabled Simon to customize his stories for the group's mood and answer questions in more detail.

Vic hung back, smiling and polite, but to Simon's eye, clearly on guard without trying to look like it. That told Simon more than any words just how concerned Vic was about everything that had been going on.

Dante kept up a running commentary in Simon's head, feeding him answers to questions. The ghost dropped little tidbits of information that even pirate scholars would be hard-pressed to know because they were not the kind of details anyone at the time would have written down.

"I don't know where you get your information, but you're the most well-informed ghost tour guide we've ever had," an older man told Simon.

Simon smiled. "I draw on a lot of personal accounts—journals, letters, that kind of thing. It's almost like having someone from the period telling you all their secrets."

"*Ha, ha. Very funny,*" Dante said in Simon's mind. "*I feel like a ghostwriter. Get it? Ghost-writer?*"

"*Over two hundred years old, and your jokes still aren't funny.*"

Simon finished up, reminded the guests to come back and try their other tours, and accepted the tips customers pressed into his hand with their thanks. When he turned around, he realized that Vic was gone.

He watched the guests scatter, heading back to their cars or walking down the boardwalk. Simon went to the store, where Pete was ringing up the last customers for the night. Vic wasn't inside.

"Did you see Vic?"

Pete looked up. "He took off like he'd seen a ghost—pardon the pun. Headed toward the pier."

"Do you know what he might have seen?"

Pete shook his head. "I was busy with clients. I only looked up in time to see him run off."

Just as Simon stepped back outside, he saw Vic come jogging up. "I lost him," Vic announced and swore under his breath.

"Who?"

"I swear I saw Bert Judd, watching from a distance—which was why I wanted to come tonight."

"Here, I thought you just wanted to hang out longer, and you were on bodyguard duty."

"Can't it be both?"

"Of course." Simon took Vic's hand. "What happened?"

Vic shook his head. "He ran into a bar, and I lost him in the crowd. Whatever reason he had for being here, it wasn't good."

Simon led Vic back into the shop and looked at Pete. "Did we get any weird packages or letters?"

"Nothing but bills in the mail, no packages."

Simon helped him close the store, and then he and Vic made sure Pete got on his way safely before driving back to the bungalow.

"What do you think Judd's up to?" Simon turned to Vic once they were in the car.

"He might be letting himself be seen to rattle you," Vic said.

Simon feared Vic's cop instincts were on target. "What do we do?"

Vic reached over and tightened his grip on Simon's leg. "The IT guys are cross-referencing the fan groups' members—and once we've got a list of suspects, we'll see if any of the usernames are connected to Judd. My bet is that they'll all link to him. And tomorrow, maybe we'll find what we need to put the cold case to rest— and figure out how Judd is tied into all of this."

Simon rubbed the back of his neck with his free hand. "About that—" He told Vic about his conversations with the retired reporter and Dante's reconnaissance work at the Vampire's Castle site.

"You weren't supposed to go near there without backup," Vic chided, with an edge to his voice that told Simon Vic worried about his safety.

"Middle of the day, lots of foot traffic, and I stayed outside a busy ice cream shop on the other side of the street," Simon replied. "I didn't even go into the T-shirt shop."

Vic clearly didn't like it, but Simon knew his fiancé recognized an advantage when he saw it, and Dante was their inside man.

"So Dante confirmed bodies, ghosts, and trophies? That's great. I got a text that the warrant will be ready in the morning." Vic frowned. "Just in case Judd saw you near there, I'm going to ask for a car to watch the building. So he can't go in and clean everything out ahead of us if he suspects."

"I didn't see him. And I was watching."

"Doesn't mean he didn't see you," Vic warned.

Simon couldn't help a shiver at the thought. Even if Thompson had been the one to kill the young women, Judd had seen their deaths as a reason for hero worship and had visited the shrine with their trophies. In Simon's mind, that meant Judd was just as evil—a murderer-in-training.

"I didn't mean to jeopardize anything." Simon pulled into the drive, relieved there were no reporters in sight.

Vic shook his head. "I don't think that you did. I'm just being extra-careful. And it's a huge advantage to have Dante's intel. I'll be honest—Judd freaks me out. I think he's capable of worse than he's done—look at who he picked as a role model. The sooner we're done with this mess, the better."

7

VIC

"Everything go okay last night?" Vic asked the uniformed officer when he got to the site of the old Vampire's Castle. He handed off a box of donuts and takeout cups of coffee to the two men in the cruiser.

"Quiet night. No one in or out," the driver said, happily accepting the treats.

Vic had tapped into the traffic cameras around the building and sent a feed to the uniforms so they could have a 360-degree view without leaving the safety of their car. That made him even more sure that Judd hadn't beaten them to the evidence.

Ross and John Gordon stood on the sidewalk at the rear entrance, away from the busy T-shirt shop at street level. They'd gotten permission to bring the retired detective since he knew the layout of the upper level. Simon was with them, and while they had declined Walt's request to accompany them, they had promised to fill him in once they had the evidence in their possession.

A van pulled up with the forensic team, including a crime photographer, to record everything they found.

Vic glanced around, ensuring that everyone was in place. "Let's go."

He'd swung by the precinct to pick up the warrant, which he'd presented to the landlord for the key to the closed-off second floor. The landlord had sworn that the owner of the T-shirt shop had no access to the rest of the building and that no one had been upstairs in many years.

Vic figured that the owner had a bad case of denial or was intentionally clueless. Scratches around the lock made it clear that someone had picked it repeatedly—and recently. While he doubted that the building's owner had any idea of the gruesome secrets in the old attraction, lax security was clearly the norm.

Two squad cars had taken over for the night shift, providing backup. One team stayed on the street, while two uniforms stepped up to accompany Vic and the others through what was now the storage area of the gift shop, through a door that led to what remained of the shuttered attraction. Once they had explained what was going on, the T-shirt shop opted to close for the day, a small mercy.

"This isn't going to be a normal bust," Vic told the group. "We'll sweep the space, but what's up there isn't likely to be anything regular bullets are going to stop. Gloves and booties, everyone. Body cams, too."

He saw the skepticism on the faces of the officers and the forensics squad. Everyone knew Vic and Ross worked with a psychic and solved ghost cases, but that didn't mean they completely believed the stories.

They're going to get a crash course.

"Take these." Simon opened his backpack and handed out hex bags. "Don't open them. Keep them in your pocket where you can wrap a hand around them if things get weird. They'll help to protect you."

"Define weird," Officer Jackson said.

"You'll know it when you see it," Ross replied.

"Keep these where you can grab them fast," Simon continued, handing out large salt shakers and short pieces of rebar. "Salt and iron repel ghosts. They'll come back, but you can buy yourself time."

Finally, he pulled a shotgun from the back seat of Ross's car and filled his pockets with shells, then handed off more to Vic, who did the same.

"I thought you said we couldn't shoot what's up there," Officer Mason questioned.

"I said regular bullets weren't going to help," Vic answered. "Those aren't buckshot."

"Rock salt," Simon told them. "A blast will drive off a bad spirit for a little longer. The victims' ghosts are not our enemies. It's Thompson's spirit we need to watch out for. He was a murdering son of a bitch in life, and death hasn't improved anything."

Vic saw skepticism on the other men's faces. He had been there himself and knew how hard he'd been to convince. *They'll find out.*

"Spectral energy often fries electronics," Simon warned. "So don't be surprised if your body cams don't work right or any recordings are damaged. Just so you know."

Simon looked to Vic and Ross. "Stay close. When Thompson makes his move, he'll come at me. I'll be busy trying to send him off and protect the other spirits. Dante will run interference, but it might not be enough. You'll have to cover me. I can't blast and banish at the same time."

He raised his head and looked at the others. "When that happens—the rest of you need to stay out of the line of fire."

Vic and Ross led the way with guns and flashlights in hand. Simon and Gordon came next, followed by the two officers. The forensic team waited outside for the all-clear to proceed upstairs.

"In the old days, the entrance to the castle was through the area where the shop is now," Gordon told them, remembering. "Vampire's Castle was a hot ticket for the weekend—especially around Halloween. It ran all year long. The displays never changed, so to mix things up they had different live acts in the lobby. Magicians, spooky bands, contortionists—everything was a little dark, twisted, and weird."

"And the teens loved it as much as their parents hated it," Ross said.

"Oh, you'd better believe it," Gordon responded. "The thing is, we knew we were never in danger, even when the frights or the people in costumes made us scream. We thought we were safe. Guess that wasn't exactly true."

"Thompson did his thing long after the castle closed," Vic said. "We think he worked here as a ticket-taker in college, so he knew the building well. When it closed, and no one was using the upstairs, he saw a golden opportunity."

"And Judd?"

"He was a part-time janitor, so he not only knew the building—this is where he might have first met Thompson," Ross said.

Vic knew that Simon heard the conversation, but he appeared to be focused on his gift and any forewarning it might provide. Even with the lights on, the old bulbs overhead barely chased away the shadows. Simon's abilities could warn him that danger lay ahead and let him sense the restless spirits and feel the psychic taint left behind by fear, pain, and great evil.

The landlord assured them that the power still worked. Ross threw the master switch while Vic covered him, revealing a strange tableau.

"What the everlasting fuck are we looking at?" Vic muttered, turning slowly to take in the bizarre sight.

"The best damn place to scare yourself shitless a teenager could ask for," Gordon replied. "This area—the back part of the lobby—was made to look like a rocky cliff at night. You climb stairs that feel like you were going up a mountain, and at the top are the caves."

"All the while, there's lots of sound effects and some weird lighting," Gordon went on. "The jump scares started in the caves over there," he said when they reached the top of the stairs, pointing toward large tunnels that looked like a movie set. "The tunnels were a short maze with some creepy alcoves. On the other side, you got to the front door of the 'castle.' A 'butler' met you and guided you from room to room—standard haunted house stuff, but not as gory as what they do now."

"Of course, the big reveal was the coffin room and Dracula," Gordon told them with a chuckle. "Dracula had a whole script, and then the lights went out, you saw red eyes and heard a bat squeaking, and suddenly the butler was hurrying you out the 'secret door,' and that was the end of the show. The back staircase came down to a hallway that led around to the gift shop and snack bar."

"Wow," Vic said, trying to imagine what the scene had looked like in its heyday. With all the lights on, it was easy to see the black fabric draped to hide the scaffolding and structure. Neither the performance lights nor soundboard was active, just the glaring fluorescents used by housekeeping and maintenance. "Kennywood was never like this."

Vic glanced at Simon, trying to read his expression. "What are you picking up on? Are the victims' ghosts here?"

Simon nodded, intent with concentration. "They're hanging back. Dante's here too, vouching for us."

Ross looked at Vic. "Dead Dante the privateer?"

Vic shrugged. "He's family. What can I say?"

Simon cocked his head, listening to a conversation only he could hear. "We're the only living people upstairs. But—"

"What?" Vic's intuition tingled.

"Thompson's ghost knows we're here. The victims are afraid of him. He doesn't want to give them up," Simon replied.

"They've been trapped here with his ghost all this time?" Ross's tone made his revulsion clear.

"That's what Dante says."

Vic knew he had to trust Simon and let him take the lead, but he feared the risk his fiancé faced to rid them of the malicious spirit.

"Dante will lead me to the bodies. You're going to have to talk me through how not to fuck up the evidence."

"You handle the ghost. We'll deal with the rest," Vic promised.

Simon stepped in front and headed into the "caves," carrying the shotgun. The bright overhead lights revealed imperfections that would be hidden by theatrical lighting.

The textured cave walls were painted to look like stone. Fully illuminated, Vic could see where mechanical monsters had been hidden behind boulders to pop up as unsuspecting visitors triggered hidden buttons under the flooring.

Inside the cave, the still air smelled of dust and old rot. Vic wondered how anyone could have overlooked the odor. Not as pungent as a freshly decomposing corpse, but a lingering foulness that lodged in the hindbrain and warned of death.

Simon was murmuring to himself—or probably, to Dante. Vic still hadn't gotten used to his fiancé channeling a spirit and having the ghost inside his consciousness. He trusted Dante because Simon did and because Dante had saved their lives more than once. Vic didn't know if he'd ever get used to having a ghost around, no matter how many movie nights they spent together.

"What's up?" Vic asked Simon quietly.

"Gabriella gave me a spell to lift illusions in case Thompson used any mojo to hide things."

They walked on, and Simon stopped and pointed to several spots on the fake cave walls. "Do you see the sigils?"

Vic frowned. Several red symbols marked along the sides of the passageway pulsed with an inner glow. "What are they?"

"Ed—the retired reporter—found that mark at each place a woman went missing, but he was afraid to tell the cops. Travis emailed me this morning—it's a binding mark. Thompson used it to make it hard for his target to leave the place. I'm guessing each one is personalized to one of the ghosts to make sure they stay here."

"He locked them in?"

"Yeah. The power may have faded over the years—which might be why I saw a couple of the ghosts elsewhere. But I'm betting that their spirits couldn't move on to the afterlife."

Simon paused and closed his eyes, then whispered something. The red sigils faded and disappeared.

"What did you do?" Ross asked, reminding Vic they had an audience.

"I used a cleansing litany to dispel evil. Wasn't sure it would work, but I'm glad it did," Simon replied.

They began to walk again, and Simon looked distracted as if he were listening to something. Vic wondered if that might be Dante's ghost.

"Here." Simon stopped in front of a place where the cave maze folded back on itself and pointed to a section of the wall. He didn't sound quite like himself, which confirmed Vic's hunch that Dante was with them.

Vic looked at the place where the cave was thicker because of an outcropping. A fake boulder had been pushed up against the side, and when Vic leaned over for a better view without touching anything, he saw where the wall had been tampered with. The odor, though faded, was sharper here, and Vic didn't envy the forensics team their task.

"We'll mark it," Vic said as Ross moved to put an "X" on the floor in chalk. "But before we bring the others up, let's sweep the rest of the place. I don't like the limited line of sight."

Vic dropped his voice. "Talk to me, Simon. What's up with the ghosts?"

"They're all around us, watching from a safe distance. Dante is keeping them back until Thompson's spirit makes his move."

When they emerged from the caves, they saw the grand entrance of a faux castle. The doorway loomed over them, ominous and intimidating.

The huge doors stood ajar. Vic and Ross pushed them open, revealing a once-opulent foyer.

"They really went over the top on this, didn't they?" Ross commented.

"It looked even better back in the day," Gordon replied. "Their prop and set people were good. They made it easy to forget you were inside a huge warehouse two blocks from the beach."

"Through there." Simon pointed toward a doorway that led into a parlor. Unlike the rest of the castle set, this room looked like it had been settled by a squatter. A sleeping bag, camp lantern, and a trash bin filled with soda cans and decaying cardboard suggested that Thompson had stayed here.

On a banquette by the wall, half-melted candles bookended what appeared to be a small shrine. Simon moved closer without touching anything to confirm Vic's darkest suspicions. Jewelry, watches, hair combs, and glasses taken from the victims were the mementos Thompson kept.

"Those trophies they didn't find in Thompson's apartment?

They're here," Simon told them, sounding like he wanted to throw up.

"Shit," Ross murmured. "This is the part of the job I hate."

"We still have to break the news to the families," Vic countered. "*That's* the part of the job I hate."

Simon backed away from the shrine. "Dante says there's a dungeon set where Thompson did his worst. We should go around it —crime scene." His voice sounded thick, and in the harsh blue light, he looked pale.

"That's right," Gordon confirmed. "It was an optional scene because it was truly scary. They said the torture devices were real antiques brought over from Europe. There was a 'chicken door' so people who were too faint of heart didn't have to see it."

"What's coming up?" Simon asked Gordon as they walked through a fake library and an elaborate dining room still set with plates and pieces of wax mannequins, everything thick with dust. Vic thought Simon looked twitchy, expecting an attack.

"The coffin room and the back exit," Gordon replied. "We're almost at the end."

"I don't like this," Vic muttered. "Where in the fuck is Thompson?"

"Waiting for us."

Vic and the others turned to look at Simon, who had the glassy-eyed expression he got when he saw with his gift instead of his vision.

"Simon—"

Simon shook his head. "Gotta finish this. We owe it to the ghosts. Play it like we planned, and it will all be okay."

By now Vic knew when his partner was putting on a good face. He sensed Simon's fear, but apprehension was overwritten by resolve. He realized that from Simon's perspective, this was a supernatural hostage situation, and he knew the psychic wouldn't rest until the victims had been set free.

Simon handed off his shotgun to Vic, keeping a small iron knife for defense. He pulled a canister of salt from his backpack and laid a circle around the banquette, then put a thick line across the doorway to the coffin room. He murmured something that sounded like a prayer.

"Protection spell," he whispered to Vic. "I've added protections to this room, and ghosts can't cross a salt line as long as it's intact," Simon said louder for the benefit of those who hadn't seen a medium at work.

"Doesn't that include Dante?" Ross asked.

"Dante can take care of himself. He's our scout, and right now he's keeping Thompson's ghost busy so I can get set up."

As if on cue, they heard a thump from the next room, then the sound of breaking glass.

The temperature plummeted, and an invisible power sent Simon sprawling. The ghostly form of an angry man formed from mist, matching the photographs they'd seen of Eliot Thompson.

Vic pulled the trigger and sent a blast of rock salt through the apparition. Thompson's ghost vanished, and Simon accepted Ross's helping hand to get back on his feet.

"We'll cover you," Vic said, giving Simon a quick once-over to assure he was unhurt.

Simon moved quick, laying a large circle of salt in the center of the parlor. "Officers, Gordon—please step inside the circle but don't break the salt line. Stay here until we're done. You'll be safe." He handed the canister to Gordon. "If anything breaks the circle, use this to close the openings."

Gordon looked as if he might protest, but Vic glowered, and the retired detective put his hands up in a gesture of surrender.

"Tell us what to do," Ross said, watching the doorway to the next room with a grim expression.

Simon nodded and withdrew several items from his backpack. He set out a cloth marked with symbols that Vic knew had been sewn from threads soaked in holy water and colloidal silver to serve as his workspace without altering the crime scene.

Next, he put out a shallow silver bowl etched with runes and lit four pillar candles, one at each of the circle's quarters. He added powdered aconite, juniper, sage he grew in his garden, and leaves from other protective plants, along with a disk of polished onyx and one of agate. Then he poured blessed oil over the mixture, spoke the incantation Travis had emailed him, and dropped a lit match into the mixture.

Bright purple fire leaped into the air from the bowl as the candle flames flickered wildly.

Vic ignored the gasps and whispers from the men inside the protective circle as he and Ross stepped forward to flank Simon at the doorway of the coffin room.

Thompson's ghost hurled himself at them, only to be brought up short by an invisible barrier he couldn't cross.

Vic recognized the man from old photos. Time had not been kind. Thompson was older than in his pictures, and just from his face, Vic guessed that even if the cancer hadn't killed him, drinking would have. The man's lips moved, but Vic could not hear the ghost.

"You're dead," Simon said in a level voice. "It's time you moved on."

Thompson's sneer made his rejection clear.

"We'll remove the bodies and your trophies. There is nothing to hold you. Go quietly, and I can help you cross over."

Vic could lip-read well enough to understand "fuck you."

"Then I'll have to do things the hard way." Simon's tone held cold steel.

The lights went out, plunging them into darkness. Suddenly the mock torches in the wall sconces flickered orange. Screams echoed, no less chilling for being pre-recorded. Chains rattled, hellhounds snarled, and heavy footsteps drew closer. *Shit. Thompson brought the castle to life.*

An unexpected gust of freezing air broke the salt line. Ghostly hands grabbed Simon by the jacket and pulled him across.

Without needing to think about it, Vic leaped over the line, and Ross followed. Thompson hurled Simon to the floor and went for his throat. Vic leveled the shotgun and fired.

Thompson's ghost vanished.

"Simon! Are you—"

"Behind you!" Ross shouted, swinging his rebar through the spirit as it formed behind Vic, dispelling its image.

Vic scrambled to help Simon up, grabbing his hand and yanking him to his feet before Thompson took shape again.

"Down!" Vic ordered. Ross dropped to the floor, and the shotgun thundered, deafeningly loud as he blasted the ghost that had been right behind Ross.

"Get back in the other room and fix the line," Simon told them.

"Like hell," Vic countered. "Do your thing. We've got your back."

Simon nodded and then took a deep breath and recited the banishment rite once more. Thompson kept his distance, flickering in and out too quickly for Vic to get a bead on him. Instead, he hurled one object after another at them, hard enough that they gouged the wall and kept Vic and Ross dodging.

Vic barely managed to deflect a flying goblet from striking Simon. Ross dodged a dagger that pulled itself off the display on the wall and flew right at him. *Hurry up, Simon. I don't know how much longer we can hold him off.*

The temperature dropped further until Vic could see his breath.

"What the hell?" Ross yelped, swinging his rebar like a baseball bat to knock another goblet out of the air before it could hit Simon.

"I think the cavalry arrived."

Vic caught a glimpse of Dante's ghost and fainter images of the murdered women. They swarmed Thompson, wrestling him to the ground and pounding on him with their fists.

Simon's incantation never faltered, and the pacing didn't change. He drew himself up to his full height, shoulders squared, one hand outstretched. Vic and Ross stepped closer to Simon as the other ghosts kept their killer too busy to cause trouble.

"—banished. You have no power here, no right to remain," Simon intoned. "Eliot Thompson, I abjure you by all the powers of light. Leave this place and leave this realm. Never return."

Vic saw a blood-red glow appear on the wall behind Thompson's ghost. The other spirits drew back like the tide, leaving Thompson to fend for himself. A powerful force dragged him backward, and Thompson's ghost unraveled as it fought against the pull that drew him little by little into its maw.

The screams Vic heard weren't the recorded sound effects. He had never believed in Hell, but whatever lay beyond that glow was enough to terrify the dead.

Dante and the women's ghosts weren't affected by the pull of the red portal, but they moved to the opposite side of the coffin room, well back from whatever fate awaited Thompson.

With a final piercing shriek, the last tendrils of Thompson's spirit peeled away and vanished. A second later, the red glow shrank and disappeared as well. The overhead lights came on, and the theatrical effects flicked off.

Vic felt like he could breathe freely again. The oppressive energy linked to Thompson's presence faded between one heartbeat and the next.

He barely moved fast enough to catch Simon, who dropped bonelessly toward the floor.

"There's a bottle of water and a protein bar in his bag," Vic said to Ross, who ran to fetch it and returned moments later.

Vic cradled Simon in his arms, half in his lap. His skin was cold and his breathing shallow, proof that even with the help of Dante and the other spirits, Simon had nearly overextended himself.

"Is he okay?" Ross asked as he held out the refreshments. Vic twisted off the cap and held the bottle so Simon could drink, then ripped the wrapper from the protein bar and fed it to him in small bites.

"He will be," Vic told Ross, idly stroking one hand through Simon's hair. "But it cost him a lot. Thompson's ghost must have been unusually strong to affect him like this, even with Dante's help."

"Hello? Can we leave the circle now?" Gordon called out from the other room. Vic couldn't repress a tired chuckle.

"You can come out," Ross called to the others.

Gordon and the two officers peeked through the doorway. "Are the ghosts gone?" Gordon asked, pale and wide-eyed.

Vic nodded. "Thompson won't be back. Simon wants to talk to

the victims' spirits before they move on. None of what they tell him will be admissible as evidence, but it might help to give the families closure."

He and Simon had discussed that when they laid out the plan for the attack. Vic hadn't liked the idea since he suspected Simon would be badly drained by banishing Thompson. Simon had insisted that they needed to take the statements of the victims before their bodies were moved, and the personal items Thompson had kept were taken for evidence.

Vic looked up at Ross. "He needs to rest, and then we have to finish this. Can you please let the forensics team into the caves? Just keep them away from these two rooms. I don't want him to be disturbed until we're done. As it is, I'll be lucky if I don't have to carry him out."

"Won't have to," Simon mumbled, still sounding drugged.

Vic smiled, relieved at the response. If Simon felt well enough to be mulish, Vic knew he wasn't too deeply drained.

"Gotta send them on," Simon murmured, plucking at Vic's sleeve. "Not done yet."

"I know," Vic told him, smoothing a hand down Simon's arm as much to convince himself as to steady his partner. "Just take a few more minutes. Thompson cost you a lot."

Vic expected Simon to argue. That he didn't, told Vic that Simon was feeling the effects more than usual.

Simon stirred in Vic's arms. "Alright," Vic sighed. "Are you ready?"

Simon nodded. "It'll go faster if you record me as I talk to them. I'll repeat what they say, and we'll have a record of what happened to tell the families."

Talking to those who were left behind was always the worst part, Vic thought. There had been too many times over the course of his career when he could offer nothing but condolences to a grieving family. Knowing the truth was a double-edged sword. On one hand, the living gained closure. But sometimes, it was better not to know.

Simon wobbled as he got to his feet and managed to walk to the other room. Gordon and the officers stared but gave them plenty of space as Simon headed for his backpack. Despite him giving the all-clear to leave the salt circle, they remained inside, and it was clear to Vic that Gordon had touched it up to keep them safe.

"What now?" The officers stayed back, but Gordon looked intrigued.

"Now I take witness statements," Simon replied with a smirk. "And then the victims can finally rest in peace."

Simon returned to the warded circle where the candles still flickered, Vic close behind. The whole room smelled like burned powders and candle smoke overlaying the odors of mildew and rot.

He sat in the center of the circle and reached into his bag for two thick cylinders of jade and onyx. Simon held one piece of smooth stone in each hand, which Vic knew helped ground him and restored his energy.

Vic sat just outside the circle, ready with more water and food. Ross ran interference with the officers and forensic team, letting them start the photography process several rooms away from where Simon patiently recounted the stories of each of the murdered young women.

By the end, Vic was emotionally wrung out. Ross guarded the door to keep them from being interrupted. Despite his crossed arms and stern features, silent tears streaked down Simon's face. Vic knew that Simon's show of neutrality cost him dearly, a facade he maintained to give the dead their vindication.

"When your team is done, we should get a priest to read Last Rites before anything else is done with the space," Simon remarked. "The ghosts have moved on. Once Thompson got what he deserved, and they had a chance to tell their stories, there wasn't anything else holding them here."

"When the area is cleared, we can arrange that," Vic said. "Now, I think you've had a busy enough day. Ross can supervise here. I'm taking you home."

"It's just past lunch," Simon protested as he snuffed out the candles, poured the ashes into a special container, and gathered up the rest of his workspace, putting it all carefully back in his bag. "Not over yet."

"It is for you." Vic pulled Simon to his feet, took the backpack without asking, and got under his partner's shoulder, half-dragging and half-carrying him toward the exit.

"Call me if you need me," Vic told Ross, since Hargrove was out of the office, still recovering from his near-miss. "You know where to find me."

"We've got this. Take care of Simon," Ross replied. "I'll handle the CSI folks. And by the way, you were right—body cams are all fried. Nothing but static."

"I need to go to the shop. I told Pete—" Simon protested.

"Dude, you're in no shape to go anywhere except bed." Vic had reached the end of his willingness to compromise. "I called Pete while you were in the shower this morning and told him that I thought you were 'overly optimistic' about coming into the store after we took care of the mess here. He wasn't surprised at all and told me to knock you out if I needed to so you'd rest."

"Traitor."

"Friend," Vic countered. "He worries about you. We all do. You were amazing back there," Vic told him as they limped down the steps. "But even warriors need to recover."

"Not a warrior."

Simon's slurred words worried Vic even more than his lack of coordination. He decided to call Travis Dominick as soon as Simon was safely in bed and asleep to find out how best to help his partner heal.

"You totally are," Vic assured him. "You don't need a sword or a cape to be badass. What you did this morning was pretty damn amazing."

"Thompson got away with murder," Simon protested as Vic helped him into the car. He fell asleep in the short distance back to the bungalow, proving even groggier when they arrived. Vic had to shake him back to awareness to get him into the house.

"I am not bridal carrying you," Vic muttered. "C'mon. Let's get you inside."

Vic hauled Simon straight to the bedroom and let him collapse onto the mattress. Then he picked up Simon's ankles and pivoted his body to help him stretch out, and removed his shoes.

"Sleep. I'll bring water, Advil, and a candy bar for when you wake up."

"Go back to work. I'm okay," Simon slurred.

"Yeah, you're just fine," Vic replied. "I've got a shit ton of paperwork to do, which I can fill out here just as well as at the station. Ross has the castle situation under control, and Gordon might be retired, but he knows his way around a crime scene if Ross needs backup."

He bent to press a kiss to Simon's forehead. "Get some rest. I'll be here if you need anything."

"Thanks for having my back."

Vic could barely make out the whispered words. He trailed his fingers down Simon's face and pushed the hair out of his eyes. "Always."

8

SIMON

S imon woke with what he considered a "magic hangover." There was nothing magical about his pounding head, dry mouth, and queasy stomach, but he recognized the aftereffects of pushing his gift too hard and depleting his energy.

If he had realized how powerful Thompson's ghost was, he would have brought backup, either Gabriella or Alicia Peters—one of his cousin Cassidy's friends who was a skilled medium. Simon didn't know if that would have been permitted since it was police business, but it was worth exploring the possibility for next time. *There's bound to be a next time.*

Simon rolled over and raised himself enough to swallow the pills Vic left for him and gulp down water. He ate the candy bar slowly, feeling the sugar hit his system. His phone on the nightstand buzzed, and he reached out blindly to grab it.

When he saw Travis's name, he thumbed the call open. "Hey. What do you have for me?"

"You sound awful." Travis didn't mince words. "Vic said you'd had a rough go of things."

"I went nine rounds with Eliot Thompson's ghost. Then I heard the stories of the victims and helped them pass over."

"By yourself?"

"Vic and Ross were with me and a bunch of cops."

"You know what I meant," Travis growled. "You should have had psychic backup."

"It's harder when it's police business. More hoops to jump through," Simon replied.

"That's not going to make Vic feel any better when you get seriously hurt. *When*—not if," Travis chided.

"I know. Let's figure that out another day," Simon replied. "On the bright side, you were right about the binding sigils."

"Teag did some digging on Bert Judd and called Vic with what he learned," Travis said. "He'll keep looking. Nothing gets past him."

"Did you find anything about whatever's causing the nightmares?"

"From everything you told me and what's in the lore, I'm certain your suspicion is right that it's a boo hag—a form of Alp. That's a spirit that feeds on fear and sucks the life essence from its victims by agitating them into terrifying dreams. At its worst, this goes beyond nightmares to sleep paralysis and full sensory terrors," Travis told him.

"When that happens, the victim is immobilized—trapped in their own mind with the monster—which creates a horrifying fantasy that's impossible to break free from," Travis added. "They're pinned, unable to move or fight, while the creature drains them, and they live out their greatest fears."

"Can someone control an Alp or a boo hag?"

"Not that I've seen in the lore. These are powerful, ancient creatures," Travis warned. "Before we became 'civilized,' they were one of the things we told stories about around a campfire."

"So they find victims on their own?"

"They're attracted to turmoil," Travis replied. "Like moths to a flame. If their victim is already upset, it makes the target more susceptible. And with everything that's going on where you are, you've got a lot of people who are ripe for the picking."

"How do we get the boo hag to go away?"

"I'm not sure," Travis admitted. "Short of mass therapy."

"Not likely any time soon."

"Then your best bet is iron and silver. You can't kill a boo hag, but you can weaken it enough to trap and relocate it," Travis said. "The eighties killer's case is solved. The Slitter trial won't last forever. Once things calm down, the hag will be less likely to return."

"There will always be something," Simon replied. "Do boo hags kill?"

"That's a matter of debate," Travis admitted. "The lore contradicts itself. My personal opinion is that the hag doesn't mean to kill because that cuts off a good food source. But like a parasite that's too aggressive, it can weaken a person to the point of collapse or organ failure—or torment them to suicide."

"That's not reassuring," Simon growled. He laid the phone on his pillow and flung an arm across his eyes, wishing that the ibuprofen would kick in faster.

"One other thing—I think it's likely that the form of Alp is a boo hag because you're in the Lowcountry, and they're part of the local legends. Creatures tend to have a home territory," Travis told him.

"If I can weaken it, would a powerful root woman be able to trap and relocate it?"

"Miss Eppie? Yes. There's a long tradition of using hoodoo to run off the hags. The monster is local, so the counter-magic is local, too," Travis said.

"Short of hanging out in bedrooms and watching people sleep, how do we get close enough to trap it?" Simon felt his strength fading, but he knew this was too important to let slide.

Between the cursed objects and the boo hag, the people involved in the Slitter trial were being worn thin. At this rate, it was only a matter of time before someone was seriously hurt—or killed. If going to court was delayed—or a mistrial declared—the case could linger in legal limbo, jeopardizing everything their hard work and the risks they'd taken had contributed.

"With bait," Vic said. Simon opened his eyes. Vic stood in the doorway, and Simon wondered how long he'd been listening.

"Out of the question," Simon snapped, although his voice lacked its full strength.

"It wants to come after me—so let it. Only I won't really be alone. You'll be there to swoop in and save me, my knight in shining armor," Vic replied.

"No."

"Maybe…hear him out," Travis argued.

"I am not letting Vic put himself out there as bait for a monster —again!" Simon hated how strained his voice sounded and how much stopping Thompson's ghost had depleted him.

"Simon—I'm a cop. I was willing to try to lure Judd to come after me. This isn't the first time I've helped trap a perp."

"This isn't a thief or a drug dealer," Simon argued. "If you've been listening, then you know. This is a monster. Very old. Powerful."

"Ask Travis," Vic countered, raising his chin defiantly.

"It's not up to Travis."

Simon forced himself to sit and saw the struggle in Vic's face to remain where he was instead of rushing to help.

"How else are you going to get close?" Vic challenged. Simon and his partner rarely argued, but they both could be stubborn. "You can't lure it because you need to do the woo-woo stuff. Do you feel any better about making Ross the sacrificial lamb?"

"Of course not."

"Then who? Because this creature is going to incapacitate someone soon that we can't afford to lose. We don't have time to argue about this," Vic threw up his hands in frustration.

A piercing whistle sounded from the phone, silencing the argument.

"You can't set a trap without bait, and ethics require informed consent," Travis said, now that he had their attention. "Vic understands the risks, and he's willing to help you draw out the hag. You're used to working together. You trust each other. Don't let your relationship complicate this."

Simon felt his cheeks flush at the reproof. *Travis is right. If Vic and I weren't a couple, there wouldn't be an issue. Work partners do this kind of thing all the time. Vic's willing to deal with the risks I take as a medium. I need to respect him as a cop.*

"Okay," Simon replied through gritted teeth, still hating the plan. "You're both right. I don't like it, but I don't have another idea."

"Thank you," Vic said, and Simon understood what his fiancé didn't say out loud. *Thank you for trusting me to do my job. Thank you for respecting my decision and my experience.*

Simon just hoped he could live up to Vic and Travis's estimation of his abilities.

"There's another piece to this," Simon confessed as Vic came to sit beside him on the bed and took his hand. "When I was getting the statements from the ghosts back at the Vampire's Castle, they told me that Judd had started showing up there and talking to Thompson's ghost."

Vic gave him a sharp look. "You didn't read that into my notes."

"On purpose—because I wasn't sure what to do with it. I'm still not sure."

"Judd is the Renfield?" Travis asked, referring to Dracula's minion in the old novel. "The Igor to Thompson's Dr. Frankenstein?"

"Yeah," Simon replied. "Bad case of hero worship. If I hadn't seen Thompson's ghost get ripped apart, I'd almost think Judd might be ghost-possessed."

"Influence can be just as powerful as possession," Travis replied. "Thompson set binding sigils and was able to work spells to extend his life from his victims' energy. If Judd is setting curses, he's probably got at least a flicker of talent to pull off what he's doing."

"Once we're rid of the hag, we've got to figure out how to stop Judd," Vic pointed out. "I have the feeling that as the trial gets closer, he'll do anything to disrupt it. We can't afford to have him and the hag after us at the same time."

Simon sighed, knowing that the plan was their best shot even as he hated putting Vic in preventable danger.

Vic seemed to guess his thoughts. He reached over and laid a hand on Simon's arm. "Hey. Look at me," Vic said quietly. "We know how to handle this. I trust you to have my back."

"Thanks. I trust you too."

"Keep me posted," Travis said. "And I'll let you know if Teag and I discover anything else," he added before ending the call.

Simon realized he had a missed text from Gabriella and quickly read it. "Gabriella did some asking around in the Spanish-speaking community. She turned up information on a couple of the missing women on Walt's list."

Vic took the phone and set it on the nightstand, then his lips brushed across Simon's, gentle and reassuring. "Shower, and then come eat. You'll feel better."

When Simon walked into the kitchen, Vic looked up from where he stirred a pot on the stove. Simon smelled ham and bean soup and saw a loaf of hot take-and-bake bread on the table, along with glasses of sweet tea.

"Have a seat. This is ready. The bread is still warm, and the butter's there," Vic told him.

Vic brought bowls over and settled across from Simon. They ate in silence for several minutes. After the intense session at the Vampire's Castle, Simon felt depleted and shoveled food into his mouth, even as his stomach rumbled.

"Thank you," Simon said finally, wiping his mouth. "That hit the spot."

Vic grinned. "Can I heat canned soup like a boss, or what? Sweated over that frozen bread, too."

"Doesn't matter. It was good."

Simon helped to clear the table and clean up, then they headed into the living room and settled on the couch as Vic flipped channels.

"I was thinking in the shower…"

Vic shot him a sexy smile. "Oh yeah? Anything that involves me, lube, and fingers?"

"Not this time. I was trying to figure out how to lure the boo hag."

"Not what I generally think about when I'm slippery and naked, but go on."

Simon playfully thumped Vic on the chest with the back of his hand. "Don't ruin my concentration. So here's my plan—we go to a motel."

Vic gave him a confused look. "I'd rather have sex here."

Simon narrowed his eyes. "Not for sex. To lure the boo hag. Try to keep up. If we survive, we can have sex *after*."

"Why a motel?"

Simon gestured vaguely around the room. "The bungalow is too well-warded. So's the shop. The station is too public. But if we get a room at a motel, Miss Eppie and I can hide in the bathroom until the boo hag appears, and then trap it."

"Better get a room with a big bathroom." Vic frowned. "Won't people hear us? There'll be civilians around."

Simon shook his head. "Not if we go to an *abandoned* motel."

"Congratulations. You just made our multiple serial killer case even more creepy."

Simon knew Vic's banter hid his apprehension. When they had first worked together, Simon took the quips at face value and wondered if Vic took things seriously enough. Now, he realized that Vic took *everything* seriously—often too much so, and had difficulty letting go of what bothered him. Humor was both a shield and a release.

"When do you want to do it?" Vic asked.

Simon could tell from the tension in Vic's shoulders that his partner understood the danger—and how much his life would be in Simon's hands. He reached out to twine their fingers together. "It's not too late to change your mind."

Vic shook his head. "No. It's the best option, for all the reasons we discussed. I've put myself out there to trap plenty of psycho guys with guns. This is the first time for being monster chow."

Simon winced. "We're going to do everything possible to keep you from being 'chow.'"

"I know you will. That's why I'm willing to do it. When's Miss Eppie available?"

"I sent her an email before I got in the shower. I don't know when—"

An insistent knock on the door interrupted the conversation. Simon had a good idea who he'd find on the porch. Miss Eppie stood with her fists on her hips, glaring at Simon like he was an errant schoolboy.

"Miss Eppie, please, come in—"

"Sebastian Simon Kincaide! Have you taken leave of your senses? You want me to help you trap a boo hag after you sic it on your boyfriend? Child, what *have* you been drinking?"

Miss Eppie—Ephigenia Walker—was one of the most powerful hoodoo practitioners and root women in the Carolinas. Her jewel-toned, flowing top complemented her dark skin and made her look younger than her age, which Simon guessed to be in her seventies. Under her piercing gaze, Simon felt like he'd been caught red-handed and hauled to the principal's office.

"Miss Eppie," Vic said in greeting, coming out to join them. "Can I get you some sweet tea?"

Eppie looked from one man to the other and then gave a curt nod. "Thank you—but don't think it gets you off the hook."

Simon led them into the living room, where Eppie settled into a recliner across from where they sat on the couch. "Now, how about you start at the beginning," she ordered, perching like a queen in her chair. "And you best make it mighty darn good."

He swallowed hard and took a sip of tea before telling Eppie what they knew about the boo hag and how he and Travis had narrowed the possibilities. Halfway through his story, she finished her tea and set the glass aside, then crossed her arms and cocked her head with a look that told him he hadn't completely won her support.

"—and that's how Travis and I came up with the plan," Simon finished.

For a couple of excruciating minutes, Miss Eppie sat in silence, staring at him with a glare that could punch a hole through steel. Finally, she cleared her throat and uncrossed her arms.

"Huh. It's dangerous as all get out. But I don't see how you have any other choices," Eppie said, giving her grudging approval. "You and Travis know your lore. I know boo hags. And Vic, God love you, but you might be too brave for your own good."

"Thanks—I think?" Vic replied.

Eppie slapped her knees. "Alright then. Might as well get this over with. Any reason we can't do this at midnight tonight? I need to gather some things and make a witch ball. Simon—have plenty of iron and salt ready and your shotgun." She looked at Vic and grinned. "You've got the easy part. All you have to do is look pretty and fall asleep."

She stood and looked from one man to the other. "Simon—text me the address of the motel and the room number, and I'll meet you there at eleven-thirty. The veil is thinner at midnight, so we'll want everything set up by then—and make sure Vic is asleep."

Eppie bustled back to her car, all the while calling over her shoulder to remind them of important details. When she pulled out of the driveway, Simon felt like they had been in the path of a whirlwind. Her psychic energy was as formidable as her abilities and as fierce as her heart. Simon felt lucky that he and Vic were among the few she "adopted" as her family of the soul.

"Is she always like that?"

Simon knew that Vic had fewer interactions with the root woman and less familiarity with her strong personality. He'd clearly been taken aback by Miss Eppie's forcefulness, which Simon had come to see as colorful.

"Yes—unless she's upset, and then you'd better get out of her way," Simon replied.

Vic opened his mouth to say something when his phone rang, a tone Simon didn't recognize.

"Sheila?" Vic frowned. Simon felt the hair on the back of his neck prickle because getting a call from Ross's wife couldn't be a good thing. "I'm putting you on speaker."

"Vic—there's been an accident. Ross came home for lunch, and he slipped and fell. He hit his head—I'm at the hospital. He's got a concussion. And I think it's my fault for opening the mail."

Simon and Vic exchanged a look.

"Mail?" Simon had a bad feeling that he already knew the answer.

"I swear I thought it was safe," Sheila said. "Ross told me to watch out for anything strange in the mail. But it came in a brown envelope like everything we order online, and so I never suspected— I just took it out of the package and set it on the table. Figured Ross had been buying some fancy grill tools again."

"Hey, hey, hey," Vic soothed. "Slow down, Sheila. How about we meet you at the hospital?"

"Okay," she said, sounding relieved. She gave Vic the room number and promised to leave word at the desk to let them up.

"Looks like it's going to be a busy day," Simon observed. "I hope Ross is okay."

"Sounds like Judd got ahead of us, dammit," Vic muttered. "Ross is a sucker for grill toys, and if the envelope looked like it had been shipped from a familiar company, Sheila couldn't have known."

The drive to the hospital took only a few minutes. Vic checked in at the desk and was directed upstairs. They found Sheila sitting outside the nurses' station. She rose to hug them both.

"Thank you for coming. I know there's nothing you can do—"

"If we can see Ross, I can get a sense for whether there's something psychically clinging to him," Simon told her. "It's not something the doctors will pick up."

"As soon as they let us back in, you can come with me," Sheila said. "They're doing more assessments. They say he'll be alright in the long run, but they aren't sure what limitations he might have in the short term."

Vic hugged Sheila, and she sobbed for a few minutes on his shoulder. Simon knew that Vic and Ross had been partners since Vic relocated to Myrtle Beach. Ross had been willing to accept a partner who had left Pittsburgh under a cloud for claiming to have seen something supernatural during a hostage situation gone awry. They'd been fast friends ever since, which had included both men's partners.

"I'll get coffee," Simon offered, figuring that Sheila needed a chance to collect herself, and she'd feel most comfortable with Vic. When he returned in a few minutes, the two were sitting side by side and chatting. Vic had an arm around Sheila, who looked much calmer.

"Here you go—what's a hospital without coffee?" Simon told them as he passed out the cups. He took a sip, unsurprised that the java tasted as bitter as it smelled. Doctors, nurses, and orderlies bustled around them, with a low buzz of conversation and footfalls that never stopped. The ever-present smell of antiseptic curdled Simon's stomach.

"I swear there was nothing about the grill scraper that seemed off to me," Sheila told them after a few minutes. "It's one of those throwing star types that can fit different grates. That's exactly the kind of thing Ross orders all the time, and the packaging looked like the online store he likes, so I just threw away the envelope and left the scraper on the table."

Simon heard the guilt in her voice, but they'd already figured out that Judd's spell only affected the target. No matter how careful Sheila had been, nothing about the item would have triggered any warning.

"It's not your fault," Simon replied. "The spell wasn't for you, so it didn't harm you. That's how he's been able to send his items through the mail without cursing every postal worker who handles them. He's a clever bastard."

Vic looked up from where he'd been fussing with his phone. "The grill scraper was from the Bubba Connor BBQ collection. Two years ago, when they were shooting his TV show on location, Bubba slipped and fell and got a concussion. It sidelined him from taping for six months because of headaches and memory problems, but he made a full recovery. So that's likely to be Ross's course as well."

"The fanboy picks items with a history matched to the interests of the person being cursed," Simon explained. "That includes an injury that puts the target out of commission for a time or hurts them enough to send a warning."

Sheila shook her head. "Before I met you, I didn't think any of this stuff was possible."

"Welcome to my world," Simon replied ruefully.

"How do we break the curse?" Sheila asked.

"We're working on that. So far, getting over the injury has taken the natural recovery time," Vic said. "The fanboy hasn't picked anything where someone died—yet."

Sheila took hold of Vic's hand. "You've got to stop him. Not just for Ross, but to keep him from hurting—maybe killing—other people. This is bigger than just the Slitter case."

Vic squeezed her hand and released it. "One step at a time. We're working on that."

A woman in a doctor's white coat approached them. "Mrs. Hamilton? I'm Dr. Lansing."

They stood, with Simon and Vic stepping back to give her privacy until Sheila waved them forward. "These are my husband's police partners. They can hear whatever you have to say."

Dr. Lansing nodded. "Mr. Hamilton's concussion isn't his first, which makes it more serious. Head injuries are always unpredictable. Multiple injuries compound, so there's always more risk. We want to observe Mr. Hamilton overnight and make sure we've assessed his injury correctly. When he's released, you'll have a checklist of things to watch for. I have every reason to believe he'll make a complete recovery, but nothing is ever guaranteed."

"He's going to want to know when he can go back to work," Sheila replied with a wan smile. "What do I tell him? He's in the middle of an important case."

The doctor didn't look surprised. "Tell him—'it depends.'"

"He'll love that," Vic muttered.

The physician chuckled. "Why am I not surprised? Here's what I mean. If he follows the treatment plan, he'll get better faster. There's the incentive for compliance. That's the best I can offer. If he pushes too far too fast and over-extends, it'll delay his recovery and make his symptoms worse."

"Understood," Sheila replied. "Thank you. May we see him now?"

Dr. Lansing nodded. "I'm only supposed to let one person in at a time, but I'll make an exception this once. Please don't be long, and don't do anything to make him agitated. He needs rest and calm."

They thanked her and headed for Ross's room, letting Sheila take the lead.

Vic caught his breath when they saw Ross sitting up in his hospital bed. Simon steadied his partner with a hand to his shoulder.

Ross looked like he'd gone nine rounds with a champ and lost. He had two black eyes and a nasty bruise on the left side of his face. His hair had been shaved to allow for stitches, and his left arm was in a sling.

Ross's worried expression brightened when he spotted Sheila. "Hey, babe. Guess what? I still remember who you are. Good news, right?"

Sheila just shook her head as she came up to his bedside and leaned down to kiss him on the lips. "Idiot. There goes my chance to trade up."

"Aw, you love me."

"You're right. I do. I must be crazy." Sheila kissed him again. Ross's hand reached up to draw her closer, and he palmed her butt. Vic barely stifled a snicker, and Simon had to muffle his laugh.

"Before you get too inappropriate, we've got company," Sheila reminded Ross. Simon remembered that a lack of inhibitions could go with head trauma, glad Ross was among friends who didn't care.

"I always said you were klutzy," Vic said, taking the cue to move closer. "Admit it—you just wanted an excuse to get out of going to the trial."

"As long as I can walk, I doubt I'll get a pass on that," Ross replied. "I feel like I lost a prize fight and didn't even land any punches."

"By all means, go beat the ever lovin' shit out of your driveway for revenge when you get home," Vic snarked.

"Pass. I fucked up my shoulder. Don't need to break my hand too," Ross said ruefully.

Vic glanced back at Simon. "All clear?"

Simon focused his gift on Ross, attempting to see if he could pick up vestiges of the spell. "He's clear," Simon answered. "No residual magic."

Ross looked to Vic and then to Simon as Sheila sat on the side of his bed and took his hand. "I'm sorry. We don't need to have one of us out of commission, with the trial so close and all the other weird shit going on."

"Thompson's ghost won't be a problem anymore," Simon replied. "So that's one down—two to go."

Simon dug a hex bag out of his pocket and handed it to Ross. "Another hex bag—figured you didn't get a chance to bring the one I gave you before to the hospital. Keep this with you at all times. Put it under your pillow—whatever you have to do to hold onto it. It's the best I can do since housekeeping isn't going to let me put a salt circle around your bed."

Ross's eyes narrowed. "What now?"

"Simon and his buddies figured out more about the creature responsible for the nightmare epidemic. We're going to deal with it tonight, but in the meantime, there's no point in taking chances."

"Deal with it," Ross repeated. "A '*creature?*'"

"A boo hag, if you want to be specific," Simon deadpanned.

"They're real?" Ross's eyes bugged a little.

"Among other things," Vic replied. "With luck, that part of the drama will be done with after tonight."

After promising to make sure Ross heard all about their fight with the hag, Simon and Vic left Ross with Sheila and headed for the car. In the lobby, the TV news snagged Simon's attention, and he motioned for Vic to pause.

"—some questions raised about whether the more unusual parts of the William Fischer case might have been fabricated," the reporter said. Simon grimaced, recognizing him as one of the less reputable anchors who seemed willing to say anything to grab a headline.

"Business leaders have also expressed concern about holding the high-profile case here in Myrtle Beach, fearing a negative impact on the Grand Strand's reputation. They've filed a formal request to have the trial moved elsewhere, but so far the judge has refused to consider a change of venue."

"Fuck," Vic muttered under his breath. "No surprise where their priorities are, huh?"

"Come on." Simon grabbed Vic's arm and hurried him to the door. "No point in raising your blood pressure. We've got a big night ahead of us."

9

SIMON

"I didn't think they still had motels like this," Vic said as he and Simon walked into the room. The 1950s-era motor lodge looked like it should be in a Route 66 documentary.

"Technically, I guess they don't since this one closed down for good last month because the owner went bankrupt," Simon replied.

The decor colors reminded Simon of a sunset—teal, pink, and Creamsicle-orange. Beach Dreams' darkened neon sign looked period-authentic. Wall sections of white breeze blocks separated the one-story motel's doorways from the parking lot, screening the pairs of sea-foam green shellback metal lawn chairs that still sat outside each room.

The place had vintage charm, with teal and pink bathroom tile, a sunburst clock, and mid-century modern furniture. For its age, the motel had held up well, shutting down just short of its chance to become ironically trendy.

"Wow." Vic turned in a slow circle to take in the room. "This looks like my grandparents' vacation photos."

"It's kinda cute, isn't it?" Simon agreed as he set his go-bag down. He had chosen this motel because it was newly deserted, and there was a big enough bathroom that he and Eppie could wait for the hag without someone having to sit in the tub.

It seemed strange to use a family vacation motel as the place to catch a monster, but Simon and Eppie had agreed that the positive energy of the location could strengthen their magic.

Vic stepped close to Simon and pulled him into a kiss that said everything they weren't putting into words. *I know it's risky. I don't want to lose you. I need you to be okay. I love you.*

Simon combed his fingers through Vic's hair. "I won't let it get you," he said quietly. "I promise. Trust me?"

Vic leaned into another kiss. "With everything I have. You've got this. Kick it in the ass."

Simon looked at the king bed with a lime and pink bedspread of beach balls and flamingos. "Guess you ought to start sleeping."

Vic eyed the bedspread. "Those colors are going to keep me awake."

Simon pulled a bottle from his pocket. The sleeping pills would put Vic into REM sleep, catnip for the hag, and perfect for nightmares. If things went Simon's way, he and Eppie would handle the boo hag, and by the time Vic woke up, the worst would be over.

Vic lay on the bed, fully clothed, and got comfortable, then he crossed his ankles and let his hands fall by his sides.

Just in case, Simon slipped an iron knife and a canister of salt under the edge of Vic's pillow. The one thing he couldn't add was a hex bag. For the plan to work, the monster had to attack. Despite the strategy, Simon felt like he was betraying his partner's trust.

"Sleep tight," he murmured.

"Don't let the boo hags bite," Vic returned in a voice already heavy with sleep.

They had arrived even earlier than Eppie requested so Simon could scope out the motel and have the time he wanted to prepare for the evening.

He put his bag in the bathroom and took out chalk, then began to mark sigils on the walls. "It's like a roach trap—the hag comes in, but it can't leave," he muttered to himself.

Finally, he placed an infrared camera angled toward the bed

that connected to an app on his phone, giving Simon a way to keep an eye on Vic.

Simon had salt and iron in his pockets, along with his hex bag, an iron knife, and shotgun shells filled with rock salt. The gun was in the bathroom. If all went according to plan, Simon would cover Eppie while she worked the root magic necessary to bind the boo hag. If things went wrong, he had a few backup plans.

A knock on the door broke Simon from his thoughts. He checked the peephole and saw Miss Eppie outside.

She brushed past him, still as full of energy as she had been earlier in the day. Her gaze fell on Vic, and she watched until the steady rise and fall of his chest assured her he was asleep, however lightly.

"Here." Eppie handed Simon a jack ball and a mojo bag. "Take these. They're strong protection. They were made especially for you. The bag is a spirit ally. Give it a name, and keep it close. I have a set for Vic when we're done here. Can't use it now—the hag would notice. You did good," she continued, glancing around the room. Eppie took in the sigils, nodding with approval, and added red brick dust and graveyard dirt to the mixture. "Now, we wait."

"I thought you said the Veil was thinner at midnight," Simon whispered. He and Eppie had been in the motel bathroom for more than an hour, and he decided that if they ever did something like this again, he was getting a suite with a Jacuzzi for more legroom.

"It is. But creatures perceive time differently than we do. Don't be in such a hurry. It'll be along when the time is right." Eppie sounded confident, and Simon hoped she was right.

Between his worry about Vic, the tension of waiting for the hag, and copious amounts of coffee, Simon remained twitchy as the hours passed. He checked his phone frequently, assuring himself that Vic was safe.

Just after three in the morning, a flicker of motion registered on the camera. Simon felt the temperature drop, and he nudged Eppie, who had been quietly chanting and trancing.

"Let's go."

They moved silently, stepping over the salt mixture line that warded the bathroom door. Simon carried the shotgun with shells already chambered.

He stifled a gasp as he saw the boo hag. The creature looked like a skinned corpse, grotesquely stretched and elongated. It straddled Vic's sleeping form and leaned over him, mouth open to draw his energy. In the background, Eppie started her chant.

Essence is more than breath and soul, Simon realized, unable to ignore the bone-deep flash of fear. In just seconds, Vic looked pale and haggard.

The hag turned toward Simon, hissing and baring its needle-sharp teeth.

"Get off him, you bitch!" Simon pulled the trigger, blasting the boo hag with salt. Dousing the monster with salt prevented it from feeding or possessing Vic, which meant the hag would turn its malice on them.

The hag blinked out of sight, but Simon knew it would be back —driven by hunger and unable to leave the room. The creature was trapped with them until they captured it, or it defeated them.

Simon had pulled a short-handled broom from his bag and laid it across the end of the bed. Legend held the hag would be compelled to count every piece of straw, distracting it from Vic and making it vulnerable to Eppie and Simon.

Everything went well—before it all fell apart.

The hag moved toward the broom and ran a long-fingered hand across its bristles. But either the lore was wrong, or this hag had exceptional focus because it turned away with a snarl and rushed at Simon, raking its long nails down his chest and throwing him out of its way.

That meant the amulets protected his soul, but weren't a bullet-proof shield for his body. *Wish I'd known that a little sooner.*

Simon rolled and came up firing, ignoring the pain from the gashes and the blood that ran down inside his shirt. The shotgun thundered again, and the hag winked out, only to rematerialize seconds later between Simon and Eppie. He ran at the hag with his iron knife, unable to fire without hitting Eppie. She kept chanting as Simon fought to keep the hag away from her and Vic.

Each time the hag re-formed, its outline appeared fainter. But even weakened, the creature posed a deadly threat. Simon shot when he could and stabbed when he couldn't. If they didn't die, he'd be bruised from being thrown into walls and probably need stitches.

Eppie finished her incantation, then lit a strip of paper and tossed it into a round glass ball.

"Do it!" she shouted.

The boo hag's image wavered unsteadily, weakened by salt and magic.

"Be gone, foul and loathsome spirit…" Simon began the ancient banishment, glad he had memorized the words so that he could recite them without hesitation.

The hag shrieked in fury and its emaciated body twisted in unnatural ways, exposing muscle and sinew. It dove for the bed, clawing its way up the mattress, limbs akimbo like a crab and moving in a blur.

"Finish the spell!" Eppie shouted, realizing that Simon was torn between trapping the hag and keeping her away from Vic.

"…I bind and banish you by all the powers of light. Go, leave this place, and trouble us no more."

Eppie held out the glass ball. Inside it, ashes, embers, and a strange fog swirled, glowing brighter and brighter until Simon had to look away.

The boo hag screamed again and dug its clawed hands into the mattress as the power of the spell pulled it remorselessly toward the ball. Its body thinned and stretched as the orb sucked it in until the creature vanished and the globe flared with red light.

Eppie quickly sealed the opening with paraffin and pressed a binding rune into the thick wax, then wrapped the ball in spelled cloth and tucked it into her bag.

Simon sank to his knees. His head pounded, the slashes on his chest burned, and a nosebleed meant all he could smell was blood.

Vic woke with a gasp and bolted upright, eyes wide with panic.

Simon dragged himself onto the bed, trying to ignore where the hag's claws had shredded the mattress. "You're okay. We're all fine. You're safe."

Even in the dim light, Simon could see bruises starting on Vic's throat where the hag had choked him and bet there were more where she had grabbed his shoulders.

"Simon?" Vic's voice sounded scratchy, and his eyes looked haunted.

Simon crawled up to sit next to him and pulled Vic into his arms, not surprised to feel his lover cold and shaking with the after-effects of the haunting.

"You're bleeding." Vic drew back. "You're hurt." He took in the ripped shirt and smeared blood on Simon's face.

"We trapped it," Simon told him, ignoring his injuries. "The hag won't hunt here anymore."

"Good work, both of you," Eppie said from where she busily collected her things. She strode over to have a look at them, and Simon guessed she was using her abilities to triage supernatural wounds or residual shadows.

"The amulets couldn't protect you from everything physically, but they did provide a psychic shield. You're both unstained."

"Good to know." Simon was grateful, but utterly wrung out.

"Can you walk? Someone's sure to have heard the gunfire, and I don't want to be here when the police come. I would not look good in a jumpsuit," Eppie told them.

"Help me up." Vic pushed away from the bed and faltered. Simon caught him, concerned that the boo hag had drained Vic so quickly.

"Quite a pair we make," Simon made light of the way they both leaned on each other, but their sudden weakness worried him.

"You'll recover," Eppie said as if she could read his mind. "Clean the gashes and make sure to shower, eat, and drink, then sleep as long as you need to. I'll handle the witch ball and make sure this hag remains bound for a very long time."

They walked to their cars together, and Simon thanked Eppie again for her help before watching her drive away. Simon let Vic have his pride to limp unassisted to the passenger seat, but he didn't take his eyes off his partner until Vic was safely settled inside.

"Should you drive?" Vic asked.

"Do we have a choice?"

Simon drove back to the blue bungalow, relieved once they were safe within the wardings. Despite Eppie's certainty that they hadn't been tainted by the boo hag's malice, Simon didn't feel like they had left the spirit behind until he felt the protections around them.

"You should go to the hospital. Those scratches look bad."

Simon turned to Vic. "Do you want to explain? Because I don't."

Vic sighed. "I don't care as long as you're safe."

"I've got antiseptic and butterfly bandages. I doubt I'll need stitches," Simon replied.

They hobbled into the house, but Vic stopped in the kitchen as soon as they entered and turned on the light. He didn't say anything, just stepped into Simon's space and began to touch him carefully, as if he might vanish.

"Vic—"

"Shh." Vic unbuttoned what was left of Simon's shirt and pulled it away from his body so he could see the claw marks. He slid the shirt from his shoulders, running his hands over Simon's skin, triaging his wounds.

Vic's breath caught when his fingers stopped above the gashes over Simon's heart. His gaze dropped to the pink scars where Simon had been shot by the Slitter, and his expression tightened.

"I put you in danger. You get hurt because of me."

Simon thought his heart would shatter at the raw look on Vic's face. He grabbed Vic's hand and held it over the still-seeping gashes above his heart.

"The danger was always there. But I have healed so much because of you." He willed Vic to understand. "You are the best thing that ever happened to me, Vic D'Amato. I love you with everything I have. There's nothing I wouldn't do for you."

Simon didn't know what horrors Vic had dreamed under the spell of the boo hag, but the raw emotion in his eyes threatened to break Simon.

"I love you too, so much," Vic whispered, laying his hand over Simon's. "The dreams—I kept seeing you dead. Every close call we've had, except how it could have been. I was always too late—"

"But you weren't." Simon met Vic's gaze. "You've always come for me. I know you always will. And I'll do the same. We're okay, Vic. Breathe. The hag's gone. She can't get you anymore."

Simon had rarely seen Vic this rattled, and he wondered what else the hag had made him dream that he couldn't put into words.

"Come on." Simon led him to the bathroom. "Let's clean up, and then we can sleep. We're both calling off for the morning."

Under the harsh fluorescent bathroom light, Simon satisfied his need to check Vic just as thoroughly for injuries. Aside from the bruising—and the psychological and energy damage the hag inflicted—Vic was unhurt.

Simon sat patiently as Vic insisted on cleaning and treating his wounds. He felt the love and concern in every touch of Vic's shaking hands.

Once they had showered and changed into sleep pants, they slipped beneath the covers. Vic pulled Simon close. "I want—"

"Anything," Simon promised, although he wondered if either of them were up to the challenge.

"Want to feel you. Need to forget. *Please.*"

Simon knew that they were both too spent for much, so he slid his hand down Vic's chest, pausing to stroke his nipples until they pebbled. He let his hand drift lower, down Vic's happy trail, and slid one hand beneath the drawstring waistband until he could wrap his fingers around Vic's cock.

"Like this?"

"God, yes."

They turned to face each other in the near dark, illuminated by the glow of a single nightlight. Vic slipped his hand into Simon's pants, jacking him dry and rough, almost panicked.

Simon caught his wrist and stilled the motion. "Hey. Slow down. We've got time."

He reached for the nightstand and grabbed the lube, giving them each a generous dollop. "This is affirmation—not penance," he reminded Vic and wrapped his fingers around Vic's cock.

"The hag got in my head," Vic confessed as his hand slid from base to shaft, swirled over the knob, and slid down again. "Made me see things. I—" his voice broke off in a near-sob, but he didn't slow his rhythm, and his grip was just shy of too much.

"Shh." Simon picked up his pace and pressed the edge of his thumb against the sensitive spot just below the head of Vic's cock. He dragged a nail through the slit and then made his hand a tight channel and set a steady motion.

"Come for me," Simon begged. "We both need it. Let me make it good for you."

Vic threw his head back, open-mouthed, as his climax overtook him. Simon enjoyed the sight of his lover drunk on sensation. He was hyper-aware of Vic's hold on his cock, just enough and bloody perfect.

He came seconds later, shouting Vic's name, breathless and sweaty and undeniably alive.

They collapsed in a heap, heaving for breath, high on endorphins, marveling that they had survived.

After a time, Simon collected his wits and carefully disentangled himself from Vic, who was already sleeping soundly. Simon ran a cloth under warm water and cleaned up, then came back to bed and wiped the jizz from Vic's belly. He threw the washcloth on the floor to deal with in the morning. One glance at the clock reminded Simon that dawn was only an hour away.

They woke groggy and disoriented when Simon's alarm went off. Both of them called off for the morning, promising to come in after lunch when he woke the next time, Simon knew he'd slept longer than intended. Vic had his phone in hand and glanced over when Simon stirred.

"Hey."

"Hey, yourself."

"Ross says he'll be back in the office on Friday. He heard back from his FBI profiler friend who looked over everything we had on Judd and says he's a perfect fit for a fanboy copycat. And Hargrove is feeling better and wants to—and I quote—'get this Slitter shit over with.'"

"Yeah?"

Vic nodded. "Detective Jackson interviewed Judge Byrnam about that cursed poker chip. She admitted to having unusual nightmares. The IT guys said they thought they'd have a digital profile by late this afternoon and an idea of where Judd might be from his logins."

Simon groaned. "So you're saying we have to get out of bed?"

Vic chuckled and kissed the top of Simon's head. "'Fraid so."

Simon headed to check in at the shop while Vic went to the police station. To his surprise, Walt rose from a nearby bench where he'd obviously been waiting.

"Pete said you'd be in around lunch, so I figured I'd wait," Walt told him. "I just wanted to thank you for finally doing right by those women who went missing. I told Ed Gallagher that his tips and instincts paid off. He said what you and Vic did will let him move on in peace when the time comes."

"Thank you for bringing the case to light and not giving up on it," Simon replied. "We looked into it because you didn't let it be forgotten. Their families can finally get closure."

"Does that mean I can interview you and Vic for an exclusive story?" The glint in the newsman's eyes made Simon chuckle.

"Let me get back to you on that," Simon told him. "I need to clear that with Vic and his boss." Usually he avoided media interviews unless they were to promote Grand Strand Ghost Tours, but Walt had led them to solve the Thompson killings, and Simon figured he deserved some of the credit.

"I'll look forward to hearing from you. See you around." Walt saluted and then strolled off down the Boardwalk.

Pete had been watching from inside the shop. "I see Walt got to say what he came to say. He's been waiting for about an hour. I offered to call him when you got here, but he said he'd rather hang out."

"He's the reason we were able to solve the eighties murders," Simon replied. "We owe him a lot."

"How are you and Vic doing?" Pete asked. "You had a busy day."

Simon sighed. "That's an understatement. But the boo hag was captured, so that's one more piece of the puzzle laid to rest. Now we just have to find Judd and stop him from sending any more cursed objects."

"Is Ross doing better?"

"He and Hargrove are going back to work, although I suspect they're both moving faster than their doctors wanted," Simon told him. "I just have the feeling that if we don't get to Judd before the trial starts, he has something big planned to derail it."

"Sounds logical. I hope the police appreciate you two." Pete went to the break room and brought back cups of coffee for both of them.

Simon cradled his with both hands, soaking up the warmth and eager for the caffeine after a short night. "They do. Hargrove is a good guy. Although I don't think the city fathers are wild about us. First the Slitter trial becomes a media circus, then we unearth another serial killer. Bad for tourism."

"Getting killed isn't good for business either," Pete pointed out.

"Having a police department that's on top of these things should help to restore confidence. The city fathers forget that no vacation spot is one hundred percent safe."

"It's all about image," Pete replied. "The trial is big now, but once it's over there'll be the next headline, and people will forget. I doubt most tourists read the local news anyhow."

"I'm sorry I haven't been around as much as I should have been." Simon paid Pete well, but he didn't want to take advantage.

"You've been busting serial killers. I've got this handled."

"Thank you," Simon replied gratefully. "I hope you're right about the media losing interest. I'm ready to get back to giving tours and doing séances without seeing reporters everywhere."

The rest of the afternoon was a blissful slice of normal. Simon waited on clients, scheduled psychic readings, and enjoyed the break, knowing that there was still a storm in the offing.

His phone rang just after four. "We've got three possible locations for Judd," Vic told him. "The information the IT guys turned up dovetailed with what Teag told me when he called. Ross is back, and we're going to check them out. We've already gone by Judd's apartment—he hasn't been there in a while. Didn't show up for work, doesn't have any family. No friends that we could find."

"Co-workers who might know his habits?" Simon asked, sure Vic had already thought of it.

"The people who remembered him said he was awkward and made people uneasy. That's why he usually worked at night. Even with the janitorial company he owns, he dispatches teams to projects without interacting with them much personally. Everyone said the same thing—Judd's an odd loner and gives people the creeps," Vic replied.

"Not much to go on."

"Maybe enough if one of these locations pans out," Vic said. "With luck, I'll be home for dinner. Let's order pizza so we don't have to worry if I run late."

"Be safe."

"You, too. Go straight home and stay inside," Vic warned. "Until Judd is in custody, we don't know where he'll show up or what he'll do."

"I'll meet you at home," Simon promised. "Go get him."

10

VIC

"We've struck out twice now—third time's the charm?" Ross asked with a nervous laugh.

Vic shrugged, out of sorts. "Not surprised Judd wasn't at his house or office. We knew that. But I thought the IT guys were onto something when they gave us the log-in locations, and their info matched what Teag found."

"Judd seems to know how to play the game. If he realized he could be traced, he'd keep moving." Ross was back at work—against doctor's orders—and still looked too haggard for Vic's liking. Ross and Hargrove had argued, but given the exceptional circumstances, Vic knew their boss gave in against his better judgment.

"We've got an alert out on his license plate. He's invested in the Slitter case, so I don't think he's a flight risk. He's going to be here to 'protect' his idol. So he has to be somewhere," Vic countered.

"The IT hits are only part of the picture," Ross reminded him. "I should hear back soon as well on the real estate search. Whatever leases or purchases he has, we'll find them."

"We're running out of time," Vic fretted. "The trial is only a week away, and I'm certain Judd has some big interruption planned."

"Then we just have to stay one step ahead of him."

The IT team had traced the posting locations of the various usernames Judd had adopted in the hobby groups frequented by his victims. They had narrowed it to three aside from his house and business—a coffee shop, a diner, and a vacation cabin Judd apparently liked to frequent.

Vic and Ross had their hex bags with them. Vic also had the gris-gris bag and jack ball Miss Eppie had made for him. Some of those amulets worked their special magic with healing charms and "enhancers"—spells to heighten sight or hearing to catch wind of danger. One was supposed to deflect magic and make him "slippery"—harder to get in the cross-hairs for spells. At this point, he was willing to accept all the extra protection he could get. No one at the coffee place or restaurant had seen Judd in more than a week. Now, as Vic and Ross stood outside the cabin, Vic had to admit that the place appeared to be deserted.

"No car—and no recent tire marks, even though it's rained a lot lately," Vic pointed out. "I don't think he's here."

Ross shrugged. "We've got a warrant to look for Judd or evidence of his occupancy. Might as well go inside and see what we can find."

The small cabin had a man cave feel, and Vic wondered if it had belonged to an older relative. While the place was maintained, it showed no signs of recent occupancy.

"I'll take the kitchen." Vic stood with his hands on his hips as he did a slow turn to survey the main living area. "See if there's anything in the bedrooms."

The refrigerator was on but empty, and the lack of any garbage confirmed Vic's sense that Judd either hadn't been here or hadn't stayed long. Vic spent his time going through the desk, looking for clues to where else Judd might have gone. He took photos of the restaurant business cards and sticky note with a storage company address and found an impression of a phone number left on a notepad after the top sheet had been removed.

"Anything?" he asked when Ross returned.

"Nope. I checked the bathroom too. It looks like it's been a while since anyone was here."

"Maybe not," Vic mused. "I found an address for a storage unit. And the phone number I found on the notepad matches a campground not too far from here. He's got to be somewhere."

"He could be sleeping in his car," Ross pointed out.

"True. But we've got everyone looking for his license plate, so that isn't risk-free for him. On the other hand, hiding out at either a campground or a storage unit would make him harder to find."

"This is your little day trip, so lead on," Ross teased.

"Let's go by the storage place and the campground," Vic proposed. "We at least need to rule them out. My gut says Judd is close—he's just gotten good at hiding in plain sight."

The "Your Extra Attic" storage facility looked down on its luck. The chain-link fence was broken or bulging in places, rusted in others. The dented aluminum siding on the buildings and the weeds growing through the cracked asphalt of the parking area added to the overall impression of disrepair.

"God, I hope he's not trying to live in one of those units," Ross muttered. "I wouldn't wish that on anyone. They've probably got rats the size of St. Bernards."

The grimy handle on the dirty glass door made Vic decide to bathe in sanitizer when they got back to the car. A bored young man looked up from the computer, and Vic would have bet money the guy was watching porn instead of working.

"Police." Vic flashed his badge. "We need access to a unit rented to Bert Judd. Can you tell us which one that is?"

The man blinked slowly and looked back at the computer. Vic thought he was going to completely ignore them or demand a warrant, which they should have pursued, but apparently having the police show up wasn't unusual. Vic knew that without a warrant, he couldn't use anything in the locker as evidence.

"Unit 241. He hasn't paid the rent in three months, so you're free and clear to check it out. The locker isn't his any longer. We'll auction off everything that's left in it pretty soon."

"Got bolt cutters?" Ross asked.

The desk clerk reached beneath the counter and pulled out a long-handled tool that looked like it had seen a lot of use. "Knock yourselves out—just bring them back."

Vic and Ross took the cutters and cautiously made their way between the long buildings. Ross cut the cheap lock. Vic pulled up the rolling metal door while Ross watched his back, gun drawn.

Vic tensed, ready for trouble, and shone his flashlight into the dark interior. A crummy cot and stained bedding told them Judd had been living here not too long ago by the look of the garbage that littered the floor.

"Fuck. We missed him," Ross muttered. Vic walked inside, kicking at the refuse to see what Judd left behind.

"Not by much." Vic bent down to look more closely at a receipt clipped to a take-out bag from a fast-food restaurant. "This has last week's date."

"How did the office manager not realize Judd was living in the unit he quit paying for?"

Vic rolled his eyes. "Seriously? That guy never looks up from his porn. He's not getting paid enough to care."

"They're not going to make anything back from an auction." Ross shook his head as he looked around the barren, trash-filled unit.

"They don't know that yet," Vic replied. "Judd knew he hadn't paid his bill and was living on borrowed time. Since the grace period was running out, he bailed."

"If he couldn't afford the rent on his unit, do you think he'd be able to pay for a campsite?"

They stepped out, and Vic pulled down the metal door. "He saved money by not paying for anything as long as he lived here. Stretched his funds. So he's probably got enough for a couple of weeks' rent."

"A campground would have showers and toilets," Ross replied, wrinkling his nose at the smell.

"That too."

Vic left the cutter on the office counter. The desk guy wasn't in sight, although the door had been unlocked and the computers were still running. Then he heard a moan from the direction of the bath-room and figured the guy was "following up" on what he'd been watching earlier.

When Vic got back in the car, he squeezed a generous dollop of sanitizer into his palm and scrubbed his hands. "I need a *Silkwood* shower."

"Should have worn a hazmat suit," Ross replied, doing the same.

"If Judd's not at the campground, then we've lost him. Fuck!" Vic slapped his hands on the armrests.

"Let's go see what we find. As you said—he has to be somewhere."

Vic was surprised when they pulled into the campground. Unlike the decrepit storage unit, this place looked prosperous and well maintained. The large common building housed a snack bar, arcade, recreation center, and the camp office. Well-tended flowerbeds and a few lawn ornaments gave the place a homey touch.

"I don't get it," Ross muttered as they headed toward the camp office. "Bert doesn't own a camper. He hasn't been able to blackmail anyone into lending him the money. Why would they let him stay?"

Vic looked around and spotted his answer on the other side of the compound. "They have cabins, no lease required, and a short stay wouldn't raise questions. Not a bad plan. Plenty of camouflage."

They found a woman in her early thirties behind the front desk. Unlike the hapless storage facility desk jockey, she appeared to be on the brink of overwhelm. She held a cell phone between her chin and shoulder, talking while her fingers flew across a keyboard.

Vic and Ross held off until she ended the call, then stepped forward and showed their badges. "You rent a space to this guy?" he asked, showing Judd's picture.

"He was here for about a week," she replied. "Didn't talk to anyone, but he didn't make any trouble, either. Cleared out day before yesterday. No idea where he was going."

"Was he staying in a cabin?" Vic asked.

"Number twelve, all the way at the end. He said he really needed a place to stay and didn't care about the view."

"You said he didn't make trouble. Did he do anything…unusual?" Ross followed up.

The office manager, whose name tag read *Dani*, thought for a moment. "We get all kinds through here," she said finally. "Grumpy old codgers, mid-life mavens touring the country, and families with kids on vacation. As long as everyone plays nice, we don't care. But that guy just rubbed me wrong."

"Why?" Vic leaned in, sensing Dani wanted to confide.

"Gut feeling that he might be trouble," she replied. "Women get a sixth sense for guys like that."

"Did he do anything inappropriate?" Vic hoped he could create enough rapport for her to trust them.

"No. We haven't had any complaints. Just comments that he seemed to tune into a wavelength no one else could pick up. He weirded some people out."

"He didn't happen to say where he was going?" Ross asked hopefully.

Dani shifted from one foot to the other. "He said something about a big date coming up. I thought he meant a 'date' with someone, but maybe he meant a birthday or something. When he came to pay his bill—and he did pay in full, in cash—he told me he needed to go 'back to where it started to reconnect.' No idea what that meant."

"Thank you," Vic said. "Mind if we take a look at his cabin?"

"Have at it, but the cleaning crew has already flipped it." She handed over the key, and Vic thanked her.

"Kinda cute campground," Ross remarked as he and Vic walked to cabin twelve. "Reminds me of some of the places we stopped when my parents decided we needed to do the epic road trip vacation back when I was a kid."

"How did that go?"

"About as well as you'd expect. My sister got the flu and kept throwing up. I was surly about having to leave my friends. My dad yelled a lot. I'm pretty sure my mother had a flask of whiskey in her purse."

Cabin twelve smelled of disinfectant and furniture polish. It was a freestanding hotel room with a living area, bedroom, bathroom, and a kitchenette. The tight hospital corners on the bed linens, perfectly even towels hanging from the rail, and the reset of toiletries meant that housekeeping had been thorough removing all traces of the previous owner. Vic and Ross checked under the bed, in the drawers, at the back of the closet, beneath the sink, and around the edges of the room for anything that might have been left behind.

"Shit. I've got nothing." Vic stood in the middle of the small cabin and ran his hands through his hair. *What would Simon do?*

Vic didn't have his partner's psychic abilities, but Simon had told him more than once that he believed Vic's very accurate "cop intuition" was another alternate way of knowing. Vic usually sloughed that off, uncomfortable with the idea because he knew deep down that Simon was right.

Alright. I'll give it a try. Vic closed his eyes and thought about Judd. *What did he think about coming here? Why this place? What was he feeling? And most important—where did he go?*

Vic tried to quiet his mind and listen with his intuition. What his mind supplied was probably a combination of his imagination and an educated guess.

Desperation. Feeling boxed in. Fear of failing. Doesn't want to disappoint. Underneath that, old fear of being punished for letting someone down. Odd, strange, doesn't fit in. Magic is real.

Vic opened his eyes when Ross called his name in a tone that suggested he had been calling for a while. "Huh—what?"

"I was just about to snap my fingers in front of your face," Ross replied. "Where'd you go?"

Vic ignored the question. "I think Judd is running scared. My bet is that he was an abused child and looked up to Thompson— and later, Fischer—because they held the power of life and death over their victims. Judd wanted to stop *being* a victim, and he sided with the abusers instead of the person being abused. He doesn't want to fail Fischer. So if he goes back to where it all started—"

"The old hotel shuttle depot." Ross met Vic's gaze with wide eyes. "Where teenage Judd met serial killer and bus driver Thompson and fell in love with death."

"He'd been waiting since Thompson died to find a worthy idol. Then the Slitter came along, and Judd became the ultimate fanboy, cheering him on. Maybe Judd had chances to report Fischer and didn't—something he'd probably consider a mark of loyalty."

"And Judd lives in a fantasy world where Fischer knows how much Judd's 'done' for him. Where they have a relationship. And Judd needs to show his idol that he alone can be trusted to believe in him," Ross continued, sounding like he wanted to throw up.

"It's worth checking out," Vic said and called Hargrove with an update. They went for coffee while they waited for a search warrant.

"If he's not at the shuttle office, we're back to square one." Ross took a bite of his bear claw and washed it down with coffee.

"We'll find him. He's going to stay close with the trial coming up." Vic finished his Danish and took a long swig of his latte.

Ross checked email on his phone while Vic searched for the owner of the defunct shuttle office. Having a key was nice, but kicking in the door or shooting the lock worked in a pinch—if they couldn't pick the lock.

"We're not getting in the easy way," Vic said with a grimace. "The building is abandoned because it got tangled up in a legal mess when the last owner and his business partner split up. One of them died; the other went on the run for unpaid taxes. The bank foreclosed. Hargrove's got a call in to get their okay."

"On the bright side, that means no one is going to call up and bitch to Hargrove because we ruined their door," Ross pointed out.

"Just remember the curses," Vic said. "Use gloves. We'll get Simon to look at whatever we find before we let the evidence guys have it."

Sooner than Vic expected, his phone pinged with authorization from Hargrove. "We're good to go. Bank gave permission, and we've got an emergency search warrant," he told Ross as they gathered their trash and headed to the car. Vic texted Simon with an update and told him where they were going, saying he'd fill him in afterward.

The old shuttle station was a squat, featureless brick building. Squinty glass block windows high on the walls protected it from break-ins but also limited visibility. That worked in their favor, although Vic had no idea if Judd had enough magic to set arcane alerts like the protections Simon and his friends had created around their bungalow and the shop.

The building had a back door into a narrow alley and no security cameras. Since it had been abandoned for years, Vic doubted it had working electricity or other utilities, so if Judd was here, he was camping rough.

The whole block had seen better days, and foot traffic was minimal. Two nearby buildings were also empty and for sale. That meant he and Ross were unlikely to be interrupted.

"Cover me." Vic pulled his lock pick kit from his pocket. Certain skills came in handy, and growing up in a family of cops meant that he had plenty of teachers to pass along the useful stuff no one taught at the police academy.

Vic listened for any sounds from inside while he worked, glad that the door was old and the lock hadn't been upgraded. He and Ross flattened themselves against the outside wall to avoid being backlit like targets.

"Police! We have a warrant, and we're coming in," Vic shouted. He braced for gunfire and exchanged a glance with Ross, then nodded. He swept the room with his flashlight, gun drawn.

Nothing moved. Daylight filtered through the dirty glass block windows, dimly illuminating the interior. Vic stepped inside, getting his bearings before venturing farther.

The station had one main room. A small office partitioned with cubicle walls sat in the back corner, and signs on the wall indicated two bathrooms. Rows of dusty plastic seats awaited passengers that would never return.

The powerful beams from their flashlights played over the shadowed corners and beneath the chairs. Only the small office and the restrooms were hidden from view, but that was enough to shelter Judd if he had made this his last bolt hole.

There. Vic gestured for Ross to follow his line of sight, illuminating a wastebasket filled with fast-food wrappers and soda cans. *Same brands as he left behind in the storage unit. I'm gonna bet that's not from long ago.*

He sniffed the air and picked up a whiff of fried chicken and rancid fries.

He's here. Vic met Ross's gaze and nodded.

"Bert Judd. Come out and talk. Don't make this harder than it needs to be," Vic called out.

In the silence, Vic swore he could hear his own adrenaline-fueled heartbeat. Judd was somewhere in the building, with the advantage of knowing the territory.

He shone his flashlight up, only to see stained popcorn finish sprayed on a slab ceiling. *Well, that eliminates him crawling through the ductwork.*

Vic heard mumbling from the small office. Just as he swung his gun in that direction, crippling pain exploded in his gut, driving him to his knees. Seconds later, Ross fell, writhing and moaning.

A shadowy figure stood half-hidden in the office cubicle. "You shouldn't have come here." Bert Judd stepped into the main room. Vic struggled to raise his gun, but another wave of pain hit, worse than the first, making it impossible for him to keep his gun steady enough to aim.

"None of that." Judd strode up and kicked Vic's gun out of his hand, breaking fingers in the process. He did the same to Ross and collected the weapons.

"I know who you are." Judd stood over Vic, just out of reach, even if Vic could have forced his body to move. "You're the cop who ruined everything. You and that fraud psychic." Contempt thickened Judd's tone.

"Why aren't you vomiting blood?" Judd stared at Vic and Ross. "That spell should have you bleeding."

Vic figured that the hex bag and protective amulets were

blunting the worst of Judd's magic. The pain was bad, but Judd obviously intended much worse.

"The notes and gifts I sent were just a warning," Judd continued. "I hoped everyone would get the message and drop the trial. But you didn't—so now I have to play rough."

Vic felt like he was being turned inside-out. The intensity of the pain left him panting and covered with a faint sheen of sweat. "Why?" he managed to say in a strangled voice.

"When Eliot died, I couldn't save him," Judd answered, and Vic knew he meant Thompson, his first mentor in murder. "I was weak and scared. Then I saw William Fischer—a true artist. I knew I couldn't fail like I did before. So I have to save him by stopping the trial. He'll never get a fair day in court. But I can end it—make them stop, set him free."

Vic heard the madness in Judd's voice. *If I can just keep him talking, maybe we'll figure a way out of this.*

"How?" Vic asked through gritted teeth. He heard Ross moaning in pain and wondered if they had been hit by different curses—or whether his additional amulets blunted more of the malicious magic.

"I have special spells hand-picked to punish the people who are trying to hurt William," Judd replied. "This is just one of them. The book had all kinds of ideas."

"Book?" *Keep him monologuing. If he's talking, he's not doing something worse—like killing us.*

"I watched the rituals Eliot performed when he thought no one was around. They were beautiful. I wanted to know what that kind of power felt like," Judd replied, sounding enraptured by the memory. "I found an old book at an antique store about magic, and it had rituals like those. But I didn't use them until you tried to take William from me."

As far as we can tell, Fischer never met this guy before he went to jail. Judd is living in his own private fairy tale.

"Since you're here, you can be my test subjects. My 'gut wrencher' spell seems to work. Let's see how 'skin on fire' does."

Judd mumbled words Vic couldn't quite catch. Abruptly, the

pain in his abdomen stopped, only to be replaced by the heat of a bad sunburn, one that was sure to blister. Ross cried out in pain, and once again, Vic wondered if his extra protections made the difference between tolerable and excruciating.

"Ohh…that's a good one," Judd said with a chuckle, but his expression darkened as he looked at Vic. "Why aren't you screaming?"

"Screw you," Vic managed. That earned him a kick in the ribs, and he folded in on himself.

"How will I decide who gets which spell? What for the judge, and what for the jury? Can't leave out the lawyers and witnesses. And no one will know I'm the one making it happen—no one but William. He'll know I came to save him."

"I'll know." Vic barely had breath to speak.

"Neither of you will be leaving alive." Judd's voice turned cold and mocking. "I told you—it was a mistake for you to come here."

Vic heard Judd's footsteps and lifted his head enough to see their captor pace. "I've got a couple more spells up my sleeve. This one's very showy—makes quite a statement. It'll be all over the evening news."

Once again he muttered, and Vic's burning skin cooled. Between one breath and the next, Vic felt like someone had stabbed an ice pick through his skull. He bit back a moan. Ross cried out, and Vic turned to see blood leaking from Ross's nose, eyes, and ears.

"Fancy, isn't it?" Judd gloated. "I'm so glad to get a chance to see how it works before the big day. The news channels will love it. So…visual."

"And then what?" It took all of Vic's willpower to form words when pain made it hard to think.

"If I don't lift the curse, they die," Judd shrugged. "And in the chaos and fear, the trial will be forgotten. William will go back to jail, and I'll use the spells to get him out."

Judd's crazy plan just might succeed, Vic thought. Fischer would go free, dozens of people would die, and the fanboy would be a hero in his own mind.

I could die here. I'm sorry, Simon.

"Don't expect any ghosts to rescue you," Judd told him. "I mop the floor with salt water. They can't enter. You're on your own…and you aren't looking too good."

Vic had hated hearing Ross cry out in pain, but his partner's new silence worried Vic more. Ross hadn't recovered from the cursed object, so he had fewer reserves to weather Judd's assault.

Hang on, Ross. I'll figure something out. But even as he thought the words, Vic knew he was out of ideas.

A shot broke the silence. "Let them go. I won't miss next time." Simon stood in the doorway, and with the light behind him, Vic hoped Judd wouldn't be able to tell a paintball gun from a pistol.

Judd's quiet laugh sent a chill down Vic's spine. "Simon. I wondered when you'd join the party. I saved my best curse for you." He muttered again, and Simon clutched his chest, wheezing, and then sank to his knees. He paled, eyes wide with fear and pain, and gave one awful, rattling breath before he fell backward and lay still.

"Simon!" Vic gasped. What he could see through a bloody haze froze his heart. Simon wasn't moving.

"Classic death curse," Judd said, triumph clear in his voice. "I thought I'd save it for the judge."

"Simon." Vic managed to drag himself across the floor to where Simon lay.

It's over. Judd won. And I won't be far behind Simon—wherever we're going.

Simon sat up with a gasp, his right hand clutching a medallion on a silver chain.

Judd abruptly clawed at his own chest, his hand grasping as he struggled to breathe. He went down in slow motion, falling first to his knees and then face down on the floor, where he lay still.

Vic's pain vanished. Across the way, Ross's pained groan told Vic that his partner had survived.

"Simon!" Vic knelt beside Simon and tried not to hyperventilate. "How did you—"

Relief flooded through him, making Vic lightheaded. *I saw him fall. I saw him die. How—*

Simon looked unsteady as if whatever happened hadn't gone

easy on him. He slowly unclenched his right fist, revealing the intricate sigils carved into the medallion now imprinted on his palm.

"Reversal spell, based on the Rule of Three." Simon was alive, but he didn't sound okay. His hands shook, and his voice trembled. "It meant Judd's spell didn't take—and it bounced back to him three times as strong."

"God, Simon. You *died?*"

"I got better." Simon's attempt for a Monty Python-esque accent was intended to reassure, but that didn't stop the sob Vic barely choked back.

"Too damn close," Vic snapped.

"Better me than you. I had a vision—"

Simon didn't have to finish his sentence. Vic could guess the rest. Simon had foreseen a version of the future—one where Vic got hit with the killing curse and didn't have a way to reverse it. A future where Simon arrived too late.

Simon's fingers came up to stroke Vic's cheek. "How bad are you hurt?"

"You're alive. I could dance a fucking jig." Vic pulled Simon into his arms, and they clung to each other, hearts pounding, breathing fast and shallow, clutching fistfuls of shirt to hold each other up. "Ross got hit worse. Not as many protections. We need to fix that."

In the distance, sirens wailed. "Cops and ambulance are on the way. I called Hargrove, but I knew I couldn't wait for them." Simon's hoarse voice barely rose above a whisper.

Vic didn't think right now that he could speak at all.

11

SIMON

"More steaks and shrimp—come and get 'em," Vic announced, carrying a tray from the grill to the tables set up in the blue bungalow's backyard. A wealth of side dishes had been brought by their guests—appetizers, salads, and desserts. Everyone chipped in on the entrees, preferring to hold a private celebration instead of going to a restaurant. Vic happily volunteered to do the grilling, and Simon teamed up with Tracey and Pete to organize everything else.

A white triangular canvas awning protected the side yard from sun or rain. Strands of café lights created a festive atmosphere, while a propane deck heater took the chill off after the sun set. A beach-themed playlist streamed from speakers. In the distance, Simon heard the roar of the ocean, and from where he and Vic stood, they spotted the waves through the gap between the buildings across the street.

Ross and Sheila traded stories with Tracey and Shayna over a pitcher of sangria. Pete and his boyfriend Mikki laughed uproariously at something Michelle's girlfriend said as they knocked back shots of tequila. Captain Hargrove and his wife were deep in conversation with Miss Eppie and Gabriella, fortified with glasses of Merlot.

Simon slipped an arm around Vic, who leaned into him. "We made it," he said, pulling Vic close. They were both still dealing with the aftereffects of the fight with Judd—as if they didn't already have enough PTSD to last a lifetime.

"We all did," Vic replied, angling his head against Simon's shoulder.

The Slitter trial was over, and William Fischer drew a sentence of life in prison without parole for his crimes. The members of the court targeted by Judd's cursed objects made full recoveries, and thankfully no one except Vic, Ross, and Simon knew the fanboy's darker plans.

Judd's death had been officially reported as a massive heart attack. A few favors with the coroner's office ensured that the reports matched that diagnosis, since a full explanation was out of the question.

"Tomorrow, let's lock in a date at the Train Depot." Simon treasured the way it felt to have Vic, alive and healthy, at his side. This case could have gone wrong so many times. Simon offered up a prayer of gratitude to any higher being who was listening.

"Works for me. I've got my work calendar on my phone, and Hargrove will make sure we have off on whatever dates we need," Vic replied. "Assuming, of course, he's on the guest list."

"Of course," Simon answered.

They and their friends had survived, despite the odds. A killer had been locked away, and another murderer received the rough justice his soul deserved. Two groups of victims—recent and long ago—were avenged, and their families could now move on.

And Bert Judd would never graduate to the next step of his hero worship and become a copycat killer himself.

"After the crime scene is cleared, I hear that the owner of the building wants to tear it down—'get rid of bad juju' as he put it—and build another haunted attraction on the site," Vic told him, mellow from the whiskey he'd finished not long ago.

"Good for him," Simon replied without enthusiasm. "I think I'll pass on visiting."

Vic laughed. "I figured you'd say that."

After everything that had happened, this was what Simon treasured most. Good friends, good food, good times—and Vic at his side.

"Go easy on the Jack. I've got plans for later. Whiskey dick is a cockblocker."

Vic gave an insulted snort. "As if."

Simon arched his eyebrow. "Just 'cos it didn't happen at twenty-two doesn't rule it out at thirty-two."

"Party pooper."

"Which would you rather? Getting 'overly mellow' now, or—" Simon's voice dropped to whisper an obscenely detailed proposition only Vic could hear.

"Easiest choice I've ever had to make," Vic assured him, draining the last of his whiskey and setting his glass aside. "Getting buzzed or having you ride my—"

Simon jokingly slipped a hand over Vic's mouth. "You don't have to share that with the class."

Vic playfully bit Simon's finger and shot him a flirty glance. "We've already established that I don't share." The gravel of his voice sent a delightful chill down Simon's back.

"Neither do I." Simon accepted the shiver that ran through Vic's whole body as tacit consent.

He pulled Vic in for a kiss, long and slow and full of promises. "Good thing we're getting married then, huh?"

"It's the best thing."

AFTERWORD

Myrtle Beach is one of my favorite places, so deciding which landmarks to weave into these stories is like getting to take you on a tour. Check out Brookgreen Garden if you want to see the inspiration for the (fictional) Grand Strand Sculpture Garden—it is a really beautiful place any time of year.

The Train Depot exists as an event venue based in the old station. While Vampire's Castle is fictional, once upon a time, a similar attraction called Dracula's Castle existed in the same location in the late 1970s and provided inspiration.

Simon's shop, Grand Strand Ghost Tours, is also imaginary, but it would be located on the Boardwalk a few blocks down from the iconic Gay Dolphin Gift Cove. If you visit Myrtle Beach, and I hope you do, be sure to think of Simon and Vic!

Watch for the next book in the series—*Point Blank*, coming soon!

Some of the side characters you met in this book have their own series. Travis Dominick and Brent Lawson team up to hunt demons in Pittsburgh in the Night Vigil series. Cassidy Kincaide (Simon's cousin) and Teag Logan get cursed objects out of the wrong hands and save the world from supernatural threats in the Deadly Curiosities series. Both series are written under my Gail Z. Martin pen name.

ACKNOWLEDGMENTS

Thank you so much to my editor, Jean Rabe, to my husband and writing partner Larry N. Martin for all his behind-the-scenes hard work, and to my wonderful cover artist Natania Barron. Thanks also to the Shadow Alliance and the Worlds of Morgan Brice street teams for their support and encouragement, and to my fantastic beta readers: Ashley, Carole, Chris, Jason, Lisa, Sandra, Seth, and Sherrie, plus my promotional crew and the ever-growing legion of ARC readers who help spread the word, including: Amanda, Amy, Anne, Ben, Beth, Beverly, Chandrayee, Darrell, Dawn, Debbie, Diane, Elayne, Grace, Hannah, Harrison, Janet, Juan, Kandice, Karen, Karolina, Kathy, Kendra, Kimberly, Kitty, Lexi, Manon, Marion, Mary, Rosalind, Sandy, Sarah, Sharon, Tammi, Tammy, Terry, Theresa, and Tracey, and more!

I couldn't do it without you! And of course, thanks and love to my "convention gang" of fellow authors for making road trips and virtual cons fun.

ABOUT THE AUTHOR

Morgan Brice is the romance pen name of bestselling author Gail Z. Martin. Morgan writes urban fantasy male/male paranormal romance, with plenty of action, adventure, and supernatural thrills to go with the happily ever after.

Gail writes epic fantasy and urban fantasy, and together with co-author hubby Larry N. Martin, steampunk and comedic horror, all of which have less romance and more explosions.

On the rare occasions Morgan isn't writing, she's either reading, cooking, or spoiling two very pampered dogs.

Watch for additional new series from Morgan Brice and more books in the Witchbane, Badlands, Treasure Trail, Kings of the Mountain, and Fox Hollow universes coming soon!

Where to find me, and how to stay in touch

Join my Worlds of Morgan Brice Facebook Group and get in on all the behind-the-scenes fun! My free reader group is the first to see cover reveals, learn tidbits about works-in-progress, have fun with exclusive contests and giveaways, find out about in-person get-togethers, and more! It's also where I find my beta readers, ARC readers, and launch team! Come join the party! https://www.Facebook.com/groups/WorldsOfMorganBrice

Find me on the web at https://morganbrice.com. Sign up for my newsletter and never miss a new release! http://eepurl.-com/dy_8oL. You can also find me on Twitter: @MorganBrice-Book, on Pinterest (for Morgan and Gail): pinterest.com/Gzmartin, on Instagram as MorganBriceAuthor, on YouTube at https://www.youtube.com/c/GailZMartinAuthor/ on Bookbub https://www.bookbub.com/authors/morgan-brice and now on TikTok @MorganBriceAuthor

Enjoy two free short stories set in Fox Hollow: Nutty for You - https://claims.prolificworks.com/free/r54nldjv and Romp - https://claims.prolificworks.com/free/I4lCYKli

Check out the ongoing, online convention ConTinual www.facebook.com/groups/ConTinual

Support Indie Authors

When you support independent authors, you help influence what kind of books you'll see more of and what types of stories will be available, because the authors themselves decide which books to write, not a big publishing conglomerate. Independent authors are local creators, supporting their families with the books they produce. Thank you for supporting independent authors and small press fiction!

ALSO BY MORGAN BRICE

Badlands Series

Badlands

Restless Nights, a Badlands Short Story

Lucky Town, a Badlands Novella

The Rising

Cover Me, a Badlands Short Story

Loose Ends

Leap of Faith, a Badlands/Witchbane Novella

Night, a Badlands Short Story

No Surrender

Fox Hollow Zodiac Series

Huntsman

Again

Fox Hollow Universe

Romp, a Fox Hollow Novella

Nutty for You, a Fox Hollow Short Story

Imaginary Lover

Haven

Gruff

Trash and Treasure, a Fox Hollow Novella

Kings of the Mountain Series

Kings of the Mountain

The Christmas Spirit, a Kings of the Mountain Short Story

www.ingramcontent.com/pod-product-compliance
Lightning Source LLC
Chambersburg PA
CBHW020633110726
47899CB00002B/754